D0843761

Saving the King

George & Christine Gomez

Blue Miramar Publishing

Saving the King
ISBN 978-0-9903902-0-6
Copyright © 2014

Dedication:

For the millions of Elvis Presley fans who lost the greatest entertainer of our lifetime on a sad and gloomy Tuesday night, back on August 16th, 1977.

Chapter 1

The dankness of the sweltering Memphis heat clung to his skin as he sat in the dimly lit room during the late night hours on August 16, 1977. Although the day had long passed into night and the morning hours would soon be upon him, he struggled to signal to his body that it was once again time to rest. There he sat, an overweight, middle-aged man, slumped in a large recliner, tormented by thoughts he couldn't turn off. He wore sunglasses which sat slightly askew. A bead of sweat rolled down the side of his face and disappeared into the heavy sideburn lining his jaw. He had earlier opened a window to catch a breeze, hoping to cool the heat that coursed through his body, but it had only served to let the heavy, damp air roll into the room. His chest rose and fell as he labored for each breath. His bloodshot eyes, hidden behind the dark glasses, slowly focused on the television set in front of him that cast an eerie glow throughout the room.

Silence enveloped the room as he watched a younger version of himself on the screen with the volume turned down. He held up a pistol, did his best to steady his shaking hand, and pulled the trigger. The television exploded, and shards of glass flew all over the olive green shag carpet. Next to him on a side table sat a half-finished bottle of Pepsi and four open bottles of pills. Without looking, he reached over and grabbed a handful of pills, popped them in his mouth, and washed them down with the Pepsi. He laid back his head and dropped the pistol to the floor. Drifting in and out of consciousness, his thoughts touched on scenes from his life, reminiscing about times gone by. He finally gave in to his drowsiness and passed out.

Upon hearing the shot, two men rushed into the room. They scanned the room and quickly assessed the situation, determining that the man had done no harm to himself but had delivered a fatal blow to the television. This was not the first time they'd had to pick up the pieces. They were all too familiar with the pattern. The younger of the two men was Dave Carson, who was in his mid-40s. His husky frame and determined strides gave him an air of authority as he paced the room, assessing the damage. Next to him stood Benjamin Stone, a distinguished looking black man with patches of grey peppering his short hair. They stared at the man in the chair, shaking their heads.

"Dave," Benjamin said as he began to pick up the pill bottles. "How long you think I'm gonna have this job?"

"Barrin' a miracle, not long."

"I been with Mr. Presley and his family since he bought this home. Twenty-some years it's been. I remember the day his dad hired me. I asked his dad, 'Sir, what are my duties?' He said, 'First of all, don't call me sir. And your duties, well, it'll come to ya.' And it did, until this here boy started goin' down to that dark place after his mama died. I always felt that boy never had a fear of dying, but lately here, I can almost feel his fear of living. Now I just don't know what to do."

"Me neither," Dave said as he looked around the room, making a mental note to add the television to the growing list of things that needed tending to. It was the latest on the list of casualties, joining the air conditioning unit on the wall next to it which had earlier in the day succumbed to the same fate. "I tell ya Ben, he's not long for this world. I just feel like Elvis has given up."

"I remember when this started with him," Benjamin said as he lingered on thoughts from many years ago. "He just got back from the army. The Colonel seemed like he worked that poor boy to death."

"Yeah, well, I think you're gonna have to help me get him up to his room again," Dave said while he picked up the shards of glass scattered in front of the shot-out television. "And pick up that gun so Lisa Marie won't see it."

Benjamin picked up the gun and tucked it into his waistband.

Dave and Benjamin stood on either side of Elvis and grabbed his arms, pulling him up out of the chair, each of them grunting with the effort. As they dragged him toward the stairs, Elvis began to shuffle one foot in front of the other. In this manner they navigated him through the room and up the staircase to the second floor landing, stumbling a few times along the way. When they reached the bedroom, Elvis fell on his bed in a daze. Benjamin pulled off Elvis' shoes and pulled a blanket over him. The two men had turned to leave the room when Elvis started to mumble incoherently. They looked at each other and shook their heads. Dave turned off the light, and he and Benjamin exited the room. Shutting the door had the effect of muffling the confused ramblings of the man they left behind.

* * * *

As the sun peeked between the dark curtains drawn across the windows, Elvis dragged himself out of bed and walked toward the bathroom. He suddenly grabbed his chest, which felt heavy, as if an anvil had been placed on his sternum. He felt the blood pulsating through the veins in his temples, and his vision blurred. He tried to cry out, but the pain was overwhelming and had a paralyzing effect. Oh my God, I'm having a heart attack. *Father, forgive me. Give me another chance*, were his last thoughts before the dizziness overtook him and he collapsed to the floor, losing consciousness.

* * * *

In the kitchen below, Dave and Benjamin were sitting at the table shooting the breeze and lingering over the strong coffee Benjamin always brewed first thing in the morning. Dave loved the scent of the freshly brewed coffee and loved the way it tasted with just a touch of cream and a pinch of sugar. His spoon made a slight clinking noise while he stirred some extra cream into the cup, but it was suddenly eclipsed by a loud thump above them. They stared at each other for a long moment with eyes opened wide.

"What the hell was that?" Dave said as he jumped out of his chair and ran from the room. He bounded up the stairs to Elvis' room, taking two at a time, dreading what he would find. When he reached the door to the master suite, he grabbed the knob and pushed it open, ignoring any thoughts of protocol or proper etiquette. As he feared, before him he saw Elvis, sprawled out on the floor, barely breathing. Dave yelled out to Benjamin, who had followed close behind: "Call an ambulance! Now! And keep everyone out of this room until they get here." Dave ran to Elvis' side and shook him with no response. "Wake up E! Please wake up!"

Dave forced himself to recall everything he had learned from the CPR class he recently completed. "You can do this. You can do this. Remember. What's the first step? Calm down. You can do this," he said to himself as he rolled Elvis over onto his back. He balled up his right fist, raised it high above his head and thrust it forcefully onto Elvis' chest. "Come on E. Come on man," he pleaded, but Elvis remained lifeless. He lifted Elvis' chin, and placed his mouth over Elvis'. He puffed two initial breathes into his friend's mouth, willing each breath to revive him, but still no response. He recalled with perfect clarity the next step from his CPR training and placed the heel of his left hand over Elvis' chest, covered it with his right hand, interlaced his fingers, and began compressions, counting to himself as he pumped his hands up and down, desperately trying to keep his friend alive.

* * * *

As Dave frantically worked to revive him, Elvis' spirit left his body and hovered over the scene. He could see his friend in a fierce fight to save his life. He thought how strange it was to see this scene unfold as though he were watching a movie. He wanted to tell Dave it was okay, he was fine, but he couldn't figure out how to interact with this world. All he could do was watch. Looking down at himself was different than looking in a mirror. Somehow, he was able to look at himself with a more critical eye from this vantage point. *What in the world happened to me? How did I get to this? Look at me. I don't remember lookin' like that.* He could feel himself being pulled up out of the room. *No, no, I have to stay. Dave, help me*, he thought as he was pulled out of the room.

Chapter 2

Surrounded by a fine mist, Elvis looked around in a daze. He tentatively put one foot in front of the other and began to walk through the heavy clouds which blocked the lower part of his legs and feet from his sight. The sensation was very different than any he had experienced before. His feet were lighter and he felt as though he were gliding rather than walking. *Where am I?* he wondered as he turned around, seeing nothing but the fine mist in all directions.

"Hey boy, where do you think you're going?" a voice called out, stopping Elvis in his tracks.

From out of the mist, a tall figure of a man emerged. Elvis stared at the sight and wondered where he had come from, trying to figure out if he was real or some kind of dream. *Am I dead? Is that God? An angel?* he thought, but upon further inspection, he dismissed that idea; after all, what kind of angel would be wearing a T-shirt with a Memphis Tiger on it and a baseball cap with a logo of an 'A' surrounded by a halo?

"It's this way," the mysterious man pointed.

"Where am I? Who are you? Did I just die?" Elvis asked.

"Not exactly."

"Are Mama and Jesse here?" Elvis asked, hoping that he was to be reunited with his mother and twin brother, who had died at birth.

"They're just around the corner, but you're not meeting them just yet. It's not your time."

"No, I want to see them right now," Elvis demanded.

"I know you're used to getting the royal treatment down on Earth, but that dog won't hunt up here," the angel said and laughed. "The boss tells me he's giving you a second chance. You must be one of his favorites."

At that point, Elvis decided the figure in front of him was some sort of angel or an apparition. *Maybe I am dead*, he thought. *And what is he talking about? A second chance?*

"What do you mean a second chance?" Elvis asked.

"Well, didn't you ask for it? Follow me. I want to show you something," the angel said as he placed his arm around Elvis' shoulder. Once again, Elvis felt the sensation of being pulled out of his surroundings.

The next thing Elvis saw was a bird's eye view from inside a crowded auditorium packed with thousands of screaming fans cheering for a younger version of himself who was performing on stage. He watched as the young Elvis gyrated his hips and swung his arm wildly while he finished his final song, "Heartbreak Hotel."

"You remember this?" the angel asked as they watched the action unfold in the auditorium.

"I sure do," he answered and quietly laughed at the sight of his younger self strutting around the stage. "I remember this concert at the Ryman. But Lord, I don't remember me lookin' that good. Look at me burn up that stage. Life was so good to me then. It was before Mama died."

The angel guided Elvis over the top of the crowd and lingered above a tightly packed group of fans toward the front of the stage.

Below, they could see a middle-aged man and a woman standing on either side of a young boy. The woman was holding the boy's hand protectively when the crowd started to press in from behind and push them uncontrollably forward.

"Goodnight," young Elvis said from the stage. "Thanks, Nashville."

The crowd erupted and rushed the stage. The sound was deafening, and the young boy was swallowed up by the mob as his hand slipped away from the woman, who desperately tried to maintain her grip.

"Mom! Dad!" the boy yelled out as the crowd moved him forward. "Where are you?"

"Richard!" the woman cried. "Richard!" She pushed people out of the way trying to find the boy. The man at her side started to yell at the crowd around him, "Move! Let me through! Richard!"

The angel guided Elvis over the crowd, following the boy as he pushed his way out of the mob and ended up at the side of the stage near an exit door. They watched as the boy began to cry and exited the auditorium through the door that led to the back parking lot. Elvis wanted to help the boy but was powerless to intervene. He tried to yell out to the boy's parents, "Hey, he's over here!" but no one looked his way. He reached down and tried to steer the little boy back in the direction of his parents, but as his hand neared the little boy's shoulder, he couldn't feel a connection; his hand glided right through the boy, who showed no sign of recognition that anyone had touched him.

Guided by the angel, Elvis looked down at the back parking lot. He watched as his old band packed up their gear. He was mesmerized by the scene as memories of his early career rushed his thoughts. *Look at Bill there, I miss that guy. He could sure play the hell outta that bass*, he thought while watching the bass player pack up his case into the back of a van. "Hey Bill! Bill! Look at me. Over here; it's me. Look at me!" he yelled to no avail. No one acknowledged his existence. He watched as his younger self strode toward the van, slicking his hair back with his hand and offering to help one of the roadies load up a heavy speaker. As they were lifting the speaker into place, the young Elvis cocked his head as though he might have heard the little boy's faint sobs drifting his way, but just then a group of excited young girls ran up to him, screaming and holding papers and pens up and asking for autographs. They blocked his view of the boy and drowned out the sound of his crying. Elvis' spirit continued to watch as his younger self signed autographs and as his left lip involuntarily lifted up into the trademark sneer he was so well known for.

From that vantage point, Elvis' spirit could see a black car slowly creeping up behind the young boy. The car door opened, and a man dressed in dark clothes got out and walked toward the frightened boy.

"Hey, that man's gonna grab that kid. Someone needs to help him. Why am I just signing autographs?"

The man grabbed the boy and threw him over his shoulder. The boy kicked and screamed, but the man refused to release his grip on the boy.

"You really don't remember, do ya?" the angel said.

"Remember what?"

"Just keep on watching."

A gust of wind came up, blowing the papers out of the girls' hands.

"That gust of wind was me. I needed to get your attention back to that little boy."

"Oh, it's coming back to me now," he said as it dawned on him, "I do remember it."

As the girls scrambled to pick up their papers, young Elvis noticed the boy kicking and screaming and struggling to get away from the man, who seemed determined to pull him into the car.

Young Elvis ran toward the car and yelled, "Hey, let go of that kid or you're gonna be in a world of hurt!"

The man dropped the boy to the ground, raced back to his car, jumped in, and sped off. Young Elvis bent down and looked into the boy's face. He took a handkerchief out of his pocket and wiped the boy's tears and put his hand protectively around the young child's shoulder.

"You okay little man? That guy didn't hurt you, did he?"

"No," the young boy said, and his lip quivered slightly. He pursed his lips together as if to fight back his tears. "But I can't find my mom and dad."

"Don't worry about that. We'll get them in just a sec. What's your name?"

"Richard."

Young Elvis motioned to one of his band members to come over. "Scotty, come here. I need your help. Go to the main speaker and announce we have a little man here named Richard," he said. Looking to the boy, he asked, "What's your last name?"

"Hart."

"Announce that we have a Mister Richard Hart back here looking for his parents."

Scotty went back into the auditorium, and a few minutes later he emerged, followed by the boy's parents, who looked astonished to see their son holding hands with Elvis Presley.

The woman screamed out in relief, "Richard!"

The boy ran up to his parents and hugged them with all his might. Elvis' spirit could feel the boy's emotions and remembered how safe he had always felt when his mother hugged him.

The boy buried his face into his mother's shoulder and sobbed quietly in secret, not wanting Elvis to think him a baby. The feeling of his mother's embrace and the scent of the perfume he knew so well caused a wave of warmth and relief to wash over him, from the top of his head down to the soles of his feet.

"Kinda tugs at your heart, don't it?" the angel asked.

"Sure does," Elvis' spirit replied.

"Son," the boy's father said, "Are you okay?"

"Yeah, I'm alright. This man was grabbing me and trying to pull me away, and Elvis came running, and he helped me."

The boy's father walked up to young Elvis and shook his hand.

"Mr. Presley, my name is Andrew, and this is my wife Loretta. We can't thank you enough. That was quite a scare for us. Richard told us what happened. If there's anything I can do for you, just name it."

"Aw, that's okay. Just takin' care of business," young Elvis said. "Here kid," he said as he reached into his pocket, pulled out a Buffalo nickel, and tossed it to Richard. "It'll bring ya luck."

Richard caught the coin mid-flight, and a smile lit up his face. "Thanks, Elvis."

Elvis' spirit watched as the Harts walked away, and when he saw the father take his son's hand, he thought of his own daughter. He watched Richard look back at young Elvis, who winked and pointed at the small boy. Richard smiled back and began to play with the Buffalo nickel.

"I sure hope that boy turned out okay," Elvis' spirit said.

"Oh don't you worry none," the angel said. "He turned out just fine. In fact, he's the reason the boss is giving you a second chance."

"What? I'm getting a second chance because of what I did for that kid? Mama always said if you do good to someone, that someone might come back and do good to you."

"Your mama was smart. That kid grew up to do great things. And now it's time to get you back where you belong."

As Elvis felt himself being pulled away from the scene, he tried to memorize the faces in front of him. He didn't want to leave his old friends. He wanted to talk to Scotty and Bill. As the scene was disappearing from view, he saw his old friend DJ lugging his drums up into the van and he thought, *Man, those were great times. Life sure was good. I sure do miss those guys.* The scene dissolved in front of him as he was pulled away by a great force beyond his control.

* * * *

Elvis found himself back at Graceland, looking down at his lifeless body. He could see Dave off to the side, white as a sheet, his hair plastered to his brow and sweat stains lining his T-shirt. There were two EMTs over Elvis' body. As one of them performed chest compressions, the other took his pulse. After a few moments the one performing the compressions would take a break while the other pumped an Ambu bag into Elvis' mouth. In this manner they continued to perform CPR while a third EMT monitored an IV drip that was attached to Elvis' arm.

"I'll see you in a bit," the angel said. "Go on now."

Elvis felt himself being pulled back into his earthly body. He started coughing and opened his eyes. He could feel the pounding of the EMT on his chest and wanted desperately for it to stop.

"Damn, that hurts. Knock it off. What are you doing?"

"He's back!" one of the EMTs cried out. "Let's get him to the hospital as soon as possible. Help me get him to the stretcher."

* * * *

As the EMTs pulled Elvis up onto the stretcher, Dave let out a sigh of relief and allowed himself to smile a bit, relieved that his old friend had come back and that there was still time. He raised his hand to his temple and shook his head, thinking, *It's time to call Richard.*

Chapter 3

A tall, fair-haired man with chiseled good
looks sat in a chair behind a desk in a lavish corporate office. The walls were filled with Elvis
memorabilia. The man was intent on decipher-
ing the figures in the financial statement laid
out in front of him. As was his habit, he had a
silver coin in his right hand, and he slipped it
back and forth between his fingers in a manner
that had become second nature to him and somehow had a calming effect. The name plate on the
desk read Richard Hart, and next to it was a picture of Andrew and Loretta Hart, the couple that
had been so grateful when Elvis saved their son
all those long years ago. A loud buzz from the
intercom jolted his thoughts away from the report, and the coin slipped out of his fingers and
fell onto the desk, landing face up, displaying the
worn outline of a buffalo. While he retrieved the

coin, his secretary's voice called out to him from the intercom on the desk.

"Mr. Hart, Dave Carson is on line two," his secretary announced.

"Thanks Julie, put him through," Richard said as he reached for the phone. "Hey, what's up?"

"Richard, I'm at the hospital," Dave responded. "You hear what happened?"

"Don't tell me, another overdose."

"No, not this time; he was dead for at least two or three minutes. I really thought he was gone. Thank God I took those CPR classes. I think it saved his life."

"How serious was it?" Richard said, sitting up straighter in his chair and holding the phone tighter to his ear, placing a greater importance on what Dave was saying.

"Didn't you hear me? He was dead. It's time. It's time we do this, now."

"He wasn't breathing?"

"You want me to repeat this again? Look, to quote our friend, 'It's now or never.'"

"I won't change my mind. I've told you for years, I can't be part of this."

"Damn it! This won't work without you. He was dead last night. It was a miracle he came back. Something has to be done, and quick. This is what your father worked so hard for. Can't you get that through your thick head? I was counting on you to keep your dad's promise," Dave said.

Richard put his hand to his temple and rubbed his head, looking up to the ceiling while his inner voices struggled with the decision. He was well aware that Dave was once again wielding the memory of his father as a sword in this sparring match. He tried to deflect the jab, but Dave had reached his mark and opened up an old wound.

"I just can't lose the business my dad spent his whole life building. All the good that we do for charity, the thousands of employees that would lose their jobs—I can't. Forget it!"

"I guess I'm going to have to figure this out by myself. I'm glad your father's not around to see how much of a wimp you are," Dave said, delivering another thrust in their war of words. "Your father only trusted four people in this world, and I'm one of them, and I thought you were too."

"Trusted four people? What the hell are you talking about?" Richard asked, getting more and more agitated with the conversation. "Hold on, I'll get back to you in a second."

Richard put the call on hold and rubbed the nickel between his fingers while he looked at the picture of his parents, trying his best to gather up his defenses once again.

Chapter 4

Richard's thoughts drifted back to the day before his world had come crashing down around him, before his parents were taken, and before Dave Carson became a constant thorn in his side.

He could still remember sitting in that smoke-filled club down on Beale Street. The memories flooded back to him, and although three years had passed since that night, he remembered every detail in perfect clarity—as though he were still sitting in the booth across from his best friend, Coop, laughing and joking around. He could hear the sultry, bluesy voice of the woman singing on stage, and he could feel the deep notes from the bass guitar vibrating throughout the joint. The smoke lingered in the air while he slowly sipped from the short glass half-filled with deep, golden-colored whiskey that gave him a slight burn as it hit the back of his throat.

From the corner of his eye he watched as two beautiful women approached their table, and he felt his guarded defenses come up in response.

"Are you Richard Hart?" the first woman asked.

"He's the one and only," Coop jumped in, answering in his stead.

The second woman slapped her friend on the shoulder. "I told you it was him."

"How 'bout you coming to join us at our table?" one of the women said while she seductively placed a hand on her hip and rubbed the other down her thigh.

Her friend did her best to get Richard's attention by pushing her deep cleavage in his direction. "And let us show you a better time than this guy can."

Coop started to laugh and prodded Richard to get up and go. "Are you crazy, get your ass over there," he said.

"Thanks girls," Richard replied. "But I'm actually doing just fine right here."

The girls walked away in a huff.

"Those rich ones," the first woman said to her friend. "They think they're so much better than us."

"Mmmm, mmmm, mmmm," Coop mumbled and shook his head. "Man, are you crazy? Those were some foxy chicks. If I were still single, I'd be all over that."

Richard watched as the girls slowly made their way back to a corner table, swaying their hips rhythmically to the music as though they hoped the sight of the motion might elicit a more favorable response. At that moment a waitress approached his table.

"Whatever they're getting," Richard said to the waitress as he pointed toward the girls' table, feeling somewhat sorry for having rebuffed their advances, "Just put it on my tab."

"Man, you must be nuts letting them walk away. Those girls are hot to trot," Coop said as he admired the view of the women from behind.

"They sure were, but those girls only wanted one thing, and the color is green. And that's not what I'm looking for."

There was a time not long ago when Richard would have succumbed to their advances, but he had grown weary of spending time with women like that, having experienced one too many gold diggers during his college years at Vanderbilt.

From across the room, Richard spotted Mr. Carlisle, the family lawyer, motioning for him to come over and join him near the entrance to the club. He could tell by the somber look on Carlisle's face that something was wrong.

"Hey Coop, something's wrong here. I'll be right back."

Richard wound his way through the crowded club, eventually arriving at Carlisle's side.

"I'm glad I found you here. I was ready to give up," Carlisle said. "I've been in half a dozen blues clubs up and down this street." He paused. "Son, I'm not good at this, but I have some terrible news, and I hate that I'm the one that has to tell you," Carlisle said, and Richard could sense the man was having a hard time delivering the news. "Your parents were driving back from a charity function this evening, and there was an accident."

"Are they okay?" Richard asked, although he knew what the answer would be without asking.

A tear escaped down Carlisle's face, and his lower lip quivered as he delivered the news that shattered Richard's world into a thousand broken pieces. "No son, they're not. They were both taken away. I'm so sorry. I don't know what else to say."

Richard's knees buckled, and he began to cry. He could feel Mr. Carlisle's arm around his shoulder and was thankful for the man's attempt to comfort him even though he knew Carlisle probably had the same need for a strong, gentle hand to comfort him while he mourned the passing of his old friends.

Richard felt the strong arms of Coop pull him up from the floor.

"What do you want me to do?" Coop asked.

"Take him to Baptist Hospital, that's where he needs to be," Mr. Carlisle said.

Coop put his arm around Richard's shoulder. "Come on buddy."

Richard sat motionless, staring out the car window while Coop drove him to Baptist Hospital so he could say goodbye to the lifeless bodies of his parents. How would he be able to find his way without the two people who had always been the true north on his compass as he navigated this world?

* * * *

Richard recalled hearing on the radio the next day, "Andrew Hart, Memphis businessman and world-renowned philanthropist, was killed last night, along with his wife Loretta, by a drunk driver in a tragic automobile accident."

Three days later, Richard attended the graveside funeral of his parents. It was reserved for family and close friends and took place at the Elmwood cemetery, where work had recently been completed on the monument erected as the final resting place for Andrew and Loretta: a semi-circular marble structure with Roman columns gracing it on both sides. On that day Richard barely noticed his surroundings, being overcome by his grief, but in the years since that painful day, he had grown very familiar with every detail of this remote corner of the cemetery, having visited it often. While at the funeral, Richard had spotted a man with a familiar face standing off to the side in the shadows of the large oak trees that lined the property. Although he had seen the man many times in his father's office, he had never once spoken with him.

It was Dave Carson who stood in the shadows, not wanting to intrude on the private service, but nodding his head in sympathy when he realized that his presence had been detected by Richard.

Richard had no energy for nor any interest in introducing himself to the man or inquiring about how he knew his father. He put the thought of the man out of his mind altogether when Mr. Carlisle whispered in his ear, "I hate to bring this up today, but the reading of the will is next Tuesday in my office at 2 p.m. You need to be there, son."

Richard looked up and slowly forced himself to nod his head in agreement, replying, "Yes, sir."

Richard continued to recall the events that had unfolded following the death of his parents. He remembered what it was like to walk into Carlisle's office for the reading of the will; the secretary looked up in recognition, and Richard could see the sympathy expressed in her eyes and the slight smile that touched her lips. These were the expressions he had grown familiar with over the past few days. Everyone he greeted had the same look about them. The secretary buzzed her boss on the intercom.

"Sir, he's here."

"Take him to the boardroom and see if he needs anything," Richard could hear Carlisle direct her through the speaker.

"Yes, sir," she said. "Mr. Hart, please follow me. I just want to say how sorry I am about your father and mother. Your father always called me by my first name and told me a joke every time he came in."

"Yeah, he loved those corny jokes," Richard said, beginning to feel the awkwardness slip away as they both quietly laughed at the memory. "Thanks for that."

The secretary led Richard into a lavish room with a long table. He sat at the end of the table near a large window. The day was bright and sunny, and he could see the sun glint off the gentle waves of the Mississippi River far in the distance as it rolled lazily along its course. *This is all wrong*, he thought; *the clouds should be pressing in, and the river should be swollen and muddy, rushing along in a torrent. How dare the sun shine down on this world.*

Mr. Carlisle walked into the room and pulled Richard away from his dark thoughts.

"You ready for this?" Mr. Carlisle asked.

"I never wanted to be ready for this," Richard replied.

"We're waiting for one more person," Mr. Carlisle said as he sat down. "We'll start the reading when he gets here."

"One more person?" Richard questioned as a frown creased his forehead. He wondered who it could possibly be.

A minute later, Dave Carson walked into room. *What's this guy doin' here*, Richard thought.

"Hey, you're that guy," he said as he pointed at Dave.

"Yeah, I'm that guy."

Dave extended his hand, and Richard rose from his seat. They each grabbed the other's hand firmly in their own, both having learned at an early age the importance of a strong handshake.

"I'm Dave Carson. I can't tell you how sorry I am about the loss of your parents."

"I saw you at the funeral the other day, and I've seen you twice a week for the last year coming in and out of my dad's office. What's up with that? How did you know my dad? He never would tell me who you were."

"Well, he's gonna tell you now. Let's go sit down and listen to what your dad had to say."

After reading the opening lines of the will—"I, Andrew Hart, being of sound body and mind, do hereby put forth in writing"—Mr. Carlisle suddenly stopped and looked to Richard. "Do you want me to go over every detail, or do you just want me to tell you what's in here?"

"Just give me the highlights."

"Well basically, as you're the only heir to Andrew and Loretta Hart, you inherit everything, lock, stock, and barrel. As the vice president of his company, you'll have to step up and take the reins. I know you weren't planning on doing that for many years down the road. Sorry, I know you weren't ready for this day to be here so soon."

"I guess I don't have any choice but to be ready."

"Your dad always said that it wasn't his company that he built to greatness, it was you. He left you a letter here that he hoped you'd never have to open. He wanted you to read it in front of Mr. Carson. And now I'll excuse myself."

Mr. Carlisle handed the letter to Richard and left the room.

Richard stared at the unopened letter for a few seconds, and then looked up at Dave.

"Mr. Carson, can we go somewhere else? This building is just too depressing right now."

"Sure. Why don't we go to the square across the street?"

"Sounds good to me," Richard lied, not quite ready to feel the sun's rays shining on him again when there was no warmth to be found in his empty world.

The two men exited the office, rode the elevator down to the lobby in silence, and made their way across the street to the large park at the heart of the city. They found a bench in front of a fountain and sat down, each of them slightly nervous as Richard held the envelope out in front of him. He shook the contents of the envelope to one side, grabbed the opposite end, and ripped it open. He pulled out the single piece of paper and read the short message in silence. As Richard read the letter, Dave watched with rapt anticipation for the younger man's response. Andrew's message from beyond the grave to his son grounded both men so tightly to the moment that everything else faded away. No longer did they hear the faint sounds of the water fountain behind them, nor could they hear the playful sounds of the children playing tag nearby.

Richard stared at the words in front of him.

I need you to kidnap Elvis Presley. Dave will know when it's time. The island is ready. Everything is set up. Love you, son. —Dad

"What? You've got to be kidding," Richard said quietly to himself. Then he looked at Dave and said, "Do you know what this says?"

"Every word."

"Well then, why don't you enlighten me," he said as he stood up and nervously took out his Buffalo nickel and began to slip it between his fingers.

"He wanted to pay Elvis back somehow, in some way, but he knew money wasn't the way."

"Oh, and kidnapping is?"

"Why don't you just listen to my story first? Everything I'm about to tell you is the damn truth. If I'm lyin', I'm dyin'. Elvis and I grew up together in Tupelo. When he moved to Memphis, we lost touch for a few years. He called me up in the early '60s and said he needed some people he could trust to work for him. I was out of a job, never went to college, and by that time Elvis was the most famous man in the world, so without hesitation I said 'Hell yeah.' Elvis—I called him E—he started to depend on medications or drugs, whatever you want to call it. Started in the late '50s after his mama died, and it progressively got worse every single year. I remember one night, Vernon and I were just shootin' the bull, and he told me about how E had saved this little rich kid from bein' kidnapped sometime in the mid-50s."

"That was '56 to be exact, at the Ryman," Richard interrupted.

"Vernon told me how grateful that little kid's parents were, and I think it was then that an idea started to roll around in the back of my head. E started doin' all kinds of drugs that Dr. Nick was prescribing for him. Everyone around him was concerned. Priscilla didn't know what to do; Vernon didn't know what to do. All the Colonel cared about was makin' deals with Hollywood, cuttin' records and makin' money for everyone, especially himself. You remember all those times you saw on TV or read that Elvis went to the hospital for exhaustion? They were because he overdosed, or it had something to do with his drug abuse. Only his inner circle ever knew the truth. In the early '70s, it got to the point where Vernon and I felt he wasn't gonna make fifty. That's when I remembered what Vernon told me about your father, and I knew if anybody had the means to help Elvis, it would be him. So I can't remember when, '71 or '72, I made an appointment with your dad. I didn't think I'd be able to get in to talk with him, but I told his secretary it was about Elvis Presley, and that got me in real quick. When I walked into his office and saw Presley memorabilia lining the walls, I said to myself. 'Hell, we just might have a chance. We might can save him.' When I sat down and told your dad about everything that was happenin', he got up from his desk, pulled a chair right close next to me, and he said, 'We're gonna save his life 'cause he saved my son's life.' And that's basically how it got started."

As Dave wrapped up his story, he noticed the coin in Richard's hand. "Your dad told me about you and that Buffalo nickel."

Richard looked down at his nickel, laughed a bit, and thought back to the day he caught the coin. *This is amazing*, he thought. *Elvis saves me from a kidnapping, and now my dad wants me to kidnap him. Unreal.*

A horse and buggy trotted slowly along the street in front of them, pulling his thoughts back to what the man in front of him was saying.

"Your father and I have been setting up everything for the last few years. I'm afraid it's close to the time where we need to step in and take action. So, what do you think?"

"I had no idea my father was so into Elvis' life. Hell, I didn't even know my dad owned an island." He paused for a second as if deep in thought and then looked back up to Dave. "This is a lot for me to swallow, and it's been a long day. Let me think about it and get back with you in a few days."

"Yeah sure," Dave said, allowing his disgust to coat each word as it left his mouth, dumbfounded that Richard wasn't on board. *The nerve of this kid to question his dad's request*, he thought. "Just don't take too long."

Remembering that Richard had just lost his parents and had his own pain to deal with, Dave tapped him sympathetically on the shoulder. "Sorry again, buddy."

Chapter 5

And that was how this sparring match began, Richard thought as he focused his attention once again on the surroundings of his office and the call he had placed on hold. Dave was still on the other end, waiting for a reply. Richard looked at the photo of his parents, willing his father to speak to him and impart a word of wisdom or two as he had so often done in the past. Invisible to Richard's eye, an angel appeared in the office on the other side of his desk. If he had been able to see him, he would have been startled to see a man standing there in a Memphis Tigers T-shirt and a baseball cap.

"Dad, I wish you were here," Richard said to himself. "I need your help. What can I do? You only trusted four people? Dave was one. I was one. Mom must have been one. So who was the oth—"

Before he could finish the thought, a loud crash startled him. The angel had reached up to a photo on the wall and knocked it to the ground. Richard rose from his chair and picked the picture up from the floor. It was a photo of his father next to Johnny Cash. He lingered on it for a few seconds and got an idea. He then picked up the phone and released the hold button.

"I still don't think I can do it," he said into the receiver. "But let me get back to you in a day or two. I have to do something first."

"It better be quick."

"Talk to you later," he said as he hung up the phone. "Julie, can you come in here?" he said into the intercom.

Julie entered the room with pad and pen in hand, prepared to take dictation from the man as she so often did, but she could tell just by looking at him that something was different this time. He was pacing like a caged animal and staring at a picture of Johnny Cash, of all things.

"Call Johnny Cash in Nashville and tell him Andrew Hart's son needs a few moments with him and that it's urgent. See if he can meet me today."

"I'll get right on it."

A few minutes later she knocked on the door and walked back into the office.

"He's on music row recording today at Columbia Records. He said he'll give you all the time you need. Just show up."

"Great! Get the plane ready; I'm leaving now."

* * * *

The pilot banked slowly to the left and started his descent as they passed over the Cumberland River. The familiar sight of a small, white chapel, with its steeple peaking up from the thick trees spreading out for miles beyond the freeway below, signaled to Richard he was nearing his destination. Moments later, the plane touched down at the Nashville airport. As Richard stepped onto the tarmac, he spotted a limousine parked nearby. The driver held the door open and motioned to him.

"Is this for me? I was just going to take a taxi," Richard said.

"Yes, sir," the driver replied. "Compliments of Mr. Cash."

As they drove toward the city, Richard could hear the muffled sounds of Waylon Jennings coming from the front speakers. He slid open the divider that separated him from the driver in the front cab. "Would you mind turning that up? Can't get enough of The Outlaw."

"Will do," the driver said, turning up the volume on the rear speakers. "You want to go through the city, sir?"

"Would love to. I haven't been here for a few years. And the name is Richard. What's yours?"

"Well, my mama named me Denard, but my friends call me Deanie."

"It's nice to meet you, Deanie."

As they drove down Second Avenue, Richard soaked in the familiar scene of the clubs that lined both sides of the street. "I sure do miss all these honky-tonks," he said.

Deanie turned right on Broadway, and Richard could see the historic Tennessee theater on his left, and just beyond that on the right was the Ryman auditorium, but the sight that brought back the strongest memories came a block later as they passed the legendary Tootsie's Lounge.

"Now that place has the best Jack I've ever drunk. Can't remember how many times I left that place not remembering what I did all night," Richard said. "You know what it's like when you're in college."

"No sir, I never been, but I picked up many a stumblin' fool from these streets when I drove a taxi awhile back ago."

"I'll bet you did, and I'll bet ya a few times it was me," Richard said, and they both laughed.

A short time later, they passed his alma mater, Vanderbilt University, and on the other side of the street was Centennial Park. He recalled many a day lying on a blanket at the park studying for some test or another while soaking up the sun and marveling at the view of the immense Greek structure that sat at the top of the hill. To this day he was still amazed that a perfect replica of the Parthenon was sitting in the heart of Nashville.

From the radio, Merle Haggard's smooth baritone voice sang out the song, "Okie from Muskogee." When he reached the verse about not burning draft cards, Deanie cried out, "Damn right!"

"I take it you were in 'nam. Is that right?" Richard asked.

"101st airborne, the Screamin' Eagles. Went in the summer of '66, got back here two years later," Deanie replied.

"I was there from '67 to '68," Richard said.

They both felt their thoughts being drawn back through time to the hot, tropical jungles of Vietnam, but Merle yanked them both back to the present when he reached the chorus. They belted out the words to the song and laughed. They could both relate to the sentiments of pride in one's home state and country that was being expressed so colorfully in the song.

"I sure miss this city," Richard said. "You know Deanie, we're lucky to live in a place where you've got the greatest blues and the greatest country music all rolled into one great state. You ever been to Memphis?"

"Never been."

"Then we're gonna have to get you there."

"I heard it's a great place."

They drove down 16th Avenue and pulled into the back parking lot of Columbia Records.

"Follow me," Deanie said as he opened the car door. "We're going through the back entrance. Right here to the left," he said as they entered the building, pointing toward the door of a small recording studio.

"Thanks, Deanie," Richard said and held out a $100 bill.

"Oh, that's okay. Mr. Cash has taken care of everything."

As Deanie turned to leave, Richard said, "I'm gonna get you to Memphis one day."

"I'll hold ya to it."

Richard opened the door to the studio and saw Johnny Cash with the three musicians known as The Tennessee Three playing their instruments behind the glass of a small recording booth. Johnny was wearing earphones and standing in front of a large microphone. He was obviously singing, but from this side of the glass, the sounds of his gravelly voice could not be heard. Johnny looked up, and the two men acknowledged each other with a slight nod. When the singer finished the number, he took off the earphones and said to his band, "Alright boys, that's a wrap. See ya in the mornin'."

"Well, look at you," Johnny said as he exited the booth. "You sure have grown up, little Richard."

"Are you ever going to stop calling me that?"

"Probably not. So what's up?"

"Is there a place we can go that's a bit more private?" Richard asked, not wanting to speak in front of the band members who were packing up their gear.

"Yeah, let's go to the Ryman right down the street. I know for a fact nobody's there."

"The Ryman? You call that private? Okay, sure, I haven't been there since '56."

"Oh really," Johnny said, trying to sound surprised.

As the two men walked from the room, Johnny couldn't help but smile and nod his head, knowing the plan was playing out exactly as they'd hoped.

"I'll get Denard to drive us," Johnny said.

"You mean my old friend Deanie?"

"Yeah, Deanie." Johnny laughed, surprised to learn that Richard had become familiar with his driver on the short ride from the airport.

A few minutes later, the two men sat in the front row of an empty auditorium.

"Man, this is eerie," Richard said. "It was just like a few feet over there where I saw Elvis 21 years ago, and I got lost from my parents. This is really strange."

"So, what did you want to talk about?" Johnny asked, effectively pulling Richard back to the present.

"First of all, why were you in my dad's inner circle? Why did he trust you so much?"

"It's a long story, but basically, when I got to Memphis in the '50s, I didn't have a dollar to my name. All I owned was the shirt on my back and a guitar to strum. I started workin' part time in one of your dad's hospitals in maintenance. I got a call from his secretary that they needed someone to come up there and fix an electrical problem. I was scared half to death thinkin', *I hope I don't screw this up*. I walked in, and there he was behind the desk, drinkin' a glass of lemonade. He said, 'Want some? My wife made it, and it's good.'"

"That was his favorite drink," Richard said, and he couldn't help but laugh. "Mom always made a batch for him every morning right before he went to work."

"And it was good," Johnny said. "He kinda made me feel at ease. I fixed the problem, and he told me to sit down and we just started shootin' the breeze. That's when our friendship began. I remember one day on my lunch break, your dad walked by and heard me playin' my guitar and singin'. He stopped and said, 'Johnny, I didn't know you could sing like that. You got yourself a unique voice there. I might know just the person for you to talk to. I'll make a phone call.' And you know who that person was? Sam Phillips, head of Sun Records. What a stroke a luck it was to have crossed paths with your dad at a time when I really needed a hand up. Because of that call to Sam, I became friends with Elvis, Roy Orbison, Carl Perkins, and The Killer, Jerry Lee Lewis. So as I see it, I owe your dad my career."

"Wow, I never knew that."

"So from then on, we just became pretty good friends, even after I left the job. He'd call me from time to time just askin' me for advice, and I'd do the same with him. He called me one day and said, 'Johnny, I got more money than I know what to do with. I want to make a difference.' And I said, 'Well, why don't you build some clinics where they really need it?' I'd seen a lot a poor folks out there as I crisscrossed this country and knew they needed someone lookin' out for 'em."

So that's where Dad got the idea for his clinics, Richard thought. "I get it now. I can see why my dad trusted you so much. Look, I'm going to tell you a story, and no matter how farfetched it gets, or sounds, just go along with it. Believe it or not, it's all true."

"Can't wait for this," Johnny said.

"Ironically, the story actually started right here at the Ryman," Richard said, and then explained his dilemma in every detail to Johnny, who listened intently.

"So what do you think about all that?" Richard asked after he finished the story.

"I always knew your dad was a little eccentric, but this just takes the cake."

"I don't know what to do, Johnny. I'm kinda lost with this thing. Dad always told me you were a straight shooter. So that's why I'm here. How in the hell can I do this to Elvis Presley? What would you do?"

"What would I do? Or what do I think you should do?"

"Yeah, what do you think I should do?"

"Son, I've battled the same demons as Elvis. I needed to escape reality on a daily basis. Everything in my life came second to my addictions. If I didn't have June, I'd be in a pine box rottin' away right now. Elvis doesn't have a June in his life. So, here's what I say about this so-called plan that your dad and Dave set up."

"Dave?" Richard said, shocked that Johnny had mentioned the man's name, since he could not recall saying the name at any point during their conversation. He was fairly certain he had only referred to Dave as "an insider in Elvis' camp."

"You know Dave?" Richard asked.

"Oops," Johnny replied with a sheepish look on his face.

"Are you kidding me? I knew there was something weird about me coming here to the Ryman. You knew what my dad was planning to do all along, didn't you?"

"Well, you did say I was in his inner circle," Johnny said with a sly look on his face.

"Unreal," Richard said, at a loss for words. He couldn't help but think his dad had set even this part of the plan in motion, getting Dave to steer him toward Johnny Cash for advice. He looked around the auditorium and saw the exit sign glowing above a side door. *Right outside through that exit is where it all began. Elvis saved me that day*, he thought. *And Dad has pushed me toward this thing from beyond the grave for three years now. Alright Dad, I guess I'll give you what you want.*

"Do it, little Richard," Johnny said. He could see the wheels turning in the younger man's head and hoped the news of his part in the plan wouldn't drive Richard in the opposite direction. He held his breath and waited.

"It looks like I'll have to," Richard announced with a steely resolve. "Get ready for a massive earthquake."

"I can almost feel it now." Johnny said as he exhaled and grabbed Richard by the arm, pulling him up into a hug. "Make your dad proud. He was a great man."

"Amen to that," Richard said as he took one last look at the empty stage and imagined Elvis as he had looked back on that day in '56.

Chapter 6

The next morning Richard arrived at his office early, having come to grips with the decision he had made the day before and ready to dive in headfirst. And just as waters often feel cold and uninviting when one dives in, that's how Richard felt as he anticipated the conversation he planned to have with Dave Carson, who would be arriving at any moment. He hoped the waters would feel more familiar as he took the first few strokes on the path that he and Dave would soon be navigating together, but feared he may have entered into a rip tide from which there would be no return.

"Mr. Hart," Julie's voice came through the intercom. "He's here."

"Send him in."

"Sit down," Richard said when Dave entered the room, motioning him to a chair on the other side of his desk. "Thanks for coming in so early."

Dave looked around the office, pleased to see that all the Elvis memorabilia still lined the walls in exactly the same way they had when Andrew was its occupant.

"I've been in this office so many times. Brings me back to all those planning sessions your dad and I held within these very walls. So what's your verdict?" Dave asked, prepared to unsheathe his sword and press the man hard, wielding his words as though they were the sharp edges of the imaginary weapon he had grown so weary of carrying on his own without the man's father to help lighten the load.

"Ten to twenty," Richard said.

"Ten to twenty?" Dave questioned, and he rolled the answer around in his head trying to make sense of it. *What in the world*, he thought, not knowing how to counter this response.

"Yeah, that's what we'll get if we get caught."

"Yes! Thank you, Jesus!" Dave yelled out and mentally took his hand off the imaginary sword at his side. "So let's get to it. We need to do this as soon as possible."

"How soon are you talking about?" Richard asked.

"He's leaving in two days for his U.S. tour," Dave said, feeling the load on his shoulders begin to lift a bit, relieved to have a companion on the long, hard road they were about to embark upon. "I can set it up if I get your go-ahead."

"You think there'll be any snags?" Richard asked.

"Don't think so. Have you already taken care of the Colonel? You know, he keeps tabs on Elvis at all times."

"Not yet. I'm meeting with him in two hours," Richard said. "I called him last night and told him I had a lucrative deal regarding Elvis and that I needed to talk to him this morning. That's all it took. Don't worry about him. All he cares about is how much money is coming to him. I'll give him more than he needs. He'll be out of our hair soon enough. I can't believe I'm doing this, but I know my dad would have done the same."

"You're doing the right thing; Andrew would not have hesitated," Dave said.

"One more thing," Richard said. "Did my mom know?"

"Not at all," Dave said. "He told me he was going to keep her in the dark just in case this went horribly wrong."

"I kind of figured he would have done that. He was always watching out for us. So what's next?"

"I'll just do what I've been doin' for the last ten years. I'll pick him up in front of the house when I get his phone call. He'll get in the back seat, and then off we go, and the plan is in motion."

"Sounds good, but I'd like to check out the island first before it all goes down."

"When do you want to go?"

"Tonight."

"Not a problem."

"Okay then, meet me at my plane tonight at 8. Let's start this ball rolling," Richard said. He felt as though the troubled waters they were entering had started to warm just a bit, realizing he rather liked the man in front of him now that they were fighting on the same side.

Chapter 7

"Give me another one, Dan," Lane Bishop said as he held a glass up to the bartender. A slight slur was starting to set in which only a few of his very close friends would have been able to detect. At the top of the list of detectives would be his wife, Teresa, who had an uncanny sense for noticing even the smallest change in his manner of speech, and who would certainly be able to detect the slightest scent of alcohol on his breath.

"Alright," the bartender said, "but this will be your last one."

Lane looked at his glass and lamented, "This is your only true friend. Stays loyal to ya through thick and thin."

"Yeah, right. It stays about as loyal as your third wife did," the bartender said.

"Maybe so, but I always had the bottle to turn to. And lately I've been turning to it way too much. What time is it?"

"Little past ten."

"Shit! I gotta get home. Teresa's gonna kill me."

"You okay to drive? I'll call you a cab."

"No. I can drive. And who cares if I get caught. I'll probably sleep better in jail than I will at home tonight anyway."

* * * *

When Lane walked into the apartment, his wife, Teresa, was sitting quietly on the sofa in the shadows. She watched as he slowly opened the door and could see as he winced a bit when the hinge made that squeaky noise he had neglected to fix although she had reminded him of it often. He quietly shut the door, slipped off his shoes, shrugged the jacket from his shoulders, placed it on a nearby chair, and tiptoed toward the hall. She studied the man, feeling a deep sadness overtake her, and she had a sudden urge to get up and run her hand across the short stubble on his face. She was drawn to the man in a way she had been drawn to no other. She wanted to run her fingers through his dark, wavy hair and feel his strong arms wrap around her while she breathed in the scent of him. She wanted him to dry her tears and brush that loose hair from her face that seemed to forever be falling out of place, but she had to resist the urges inside and do what she knew was best.

"You've been drinkin' again, haven't you," she said.

Lane was startled by her voice and put his hand to his chest.

"And what if I was?" he said with a heavy sarcastic sneer. "I'm no alcoholic."

"Sure you're not," she said, not wanting to repeat the countless arguments they'd had on the subject. "All I know is for the last six months, you've been coming home late and drinking way too much. To be honest with you, our marriage is through. I'm your fourth wife. I thought I could change you, but I can't. I'm not mad; I'm tired of being mad. We barely talk. You're barely here. And this is barely a marriage."

The words hung in the air for a few moments, neither one knowing what to say next.

"Let's just call it quits," she finally said.

Lane stared at her for a few seconds, let the words sink in, and couldn't resist comparing them to similar speeches he'd heard before. He admired her ability to condense the state of their marriage into those few short lines. His last wife managed to drag out her parting speech for a couple of hours.

"I was dreading the day you were going to tell me that," he said with a heavy heart. "I'm sorry I hurt you, but you're right—this ain't a marriage."

He could see a suitcase packed next to where she sat in the shadows.

"At least you talked to me before you left. My last three never even said goodbye."

"You're not a bad man, Lane," she said as she stood up and grabbed her bag. "You've got a good heart. You just can't be settled. If you ever need anything, don't call me."

She opened the door, walked out, and closed the door on the life he had hoped they could build together. Lane took the spot on the sofa she had vacated.

"I wonder if I should start working on my fifth," he said aloud to himself, "or maybe just a fifth of whiskey."

Chapter 8

Dave was lost in thought, mentally preparing himself for what was to come later that
night. He ran down his mental checklist, noting
every detail in the elaborate plan that had to be
orchestrated with perfect timing. While he
leaned against the long, black limousine, he
stared at the white exterior of the Graceland
mansion glowing in the moonlight and admired
the slender lines of the Greek columns reaching
up to the second floor of the stately old antebel-
lum structure. The two lion statues adorning the
entrance appeared to be guarding the secrets
that lay beyond. He heard the faint tinkle of the
piano keys coming from within the walls of the
mansion. Through the front windows, which
were lined on either side with heavy, blue velvet
curtains, he could see into the living room and
beyond the stained glass panels of brilliant blue
peacocks that marked the entrance to the music

room. Within the music room, he could see Elvis sitting at the grand piano with his arm around his young daughter, Lisa Marie, who sat by his side. She wore a nightgown and protectively held a doll close to her chest with one hand while she touched the keys of the piano with the other.

From within the music room, the distinctive notes of "Twinkle, Twinkle, Little Star" could be heard as Elvis and his daughter took turns playing the notes slowly in time. Elvis loved these quiet times with his daughter. He felt somewhat guilty for having kept her up so long past her bedtime as he noticed her rubbing her eyes, barely able to keep them open, but he had been desperate to spend every last moment possible with her before he left to go on the road.

"Darlin'," he said, "I've got to go."

"I'll miss you, Daddy," she said, and she gave him a hug, lowering her doll and allowing him to take center place as she squeezed her arms around his neck.

"I'll miss you more," he said. "I'll call you every day, and I'll see you in a month. Come on," he said as he picked her up. "I'll tuck you in."

He carried her out of the small music room, through the foyer beyond, up the grand staircase, and into her bedroom at the top of the stairs. He laid her on the bed and pulled the blankets over her shoulders, tucking her in tightly on either side, hoping it would help her feel his protective presence long after he had left the room. He propped the doll next to her on the pillow, gently kissed his daughter's forehead, touched the loose, light-brown curls framing her face, and quietly laughed at how she had managed to fall asleep during the short walk up the stairs.

Dave watched as Elvis exited the doors of the mansion a short time later, noticing how overweight his friend had become. Elvis looked worn down and used up.

"Man, this is getting' old," Elvis said to Dave. "When is it gonna stop?"

"Sooner than you think," Dave said quietly to himself.

Dave closed the car door behind Elvis, walked around to the driver's side, and slid in behind the wheel. He checked off another item on his mental checklist and urged himself not to back out and to ignore the rapid pounding of his heart and the sweat that dampened his palms as he gripped the wheel in front of him.

"How you feelin', E?"

"Tired as usual. Hey, do you believe in the afterlife?"

"Yeah, why not? Sure, I believe it. Why you ask?"

"The weirdest thing happened to me when I passed out the other night and the ambulance came. I was talkin' to this guy that I think was an angel, even though he sure didn't look like one and didn't talk like one either. He showed me a concert that I did at the Ryman twenty years ago. I saw the old band there too—Scotty, and Bill, and DJ."

"Say what?"

"Yeah, I saw 'em. And he showed me something I did that I completely forgot."

"Like what?"

"Did I ever tell you about me savin' that kid from being kidnapped?"

"Yeah, I heard about it."

"I can't remember the kid's name, but the angel told me he's doin' pretty good for himself now."

Dave looked at Elvis in the rear-view mirror with his mouth opened in disbelief and laughed quietly to himself. "I'll bet he is," he replied. "I heard this guy on a talk show today talkin' about something like that, called it a near-death experience I think. Maybe you had one of those the other night."

"Yeah, maybe that's what it was. Well, anyway, forget it. It was probably just a stupid dream. Hey, do you have those pills? I need to wake up."

"They're on the plane," Dave lied, knowing full well there was a bottle in the glove box.

They travelled down the road in silence for a few minutes as Dave struggled to fight back the sick feeling rising up from the pit of his stomach.

"E," Dave said while he looked at Elvis in the rear-view mirror. "I don't know how to say this, but I'm sorry brother. I'm really sorry. I hope you don't hate me."

"What the hell you talkin' about?"

"I'm sorry man. I really am. But it's gotta be done."

Dave slowed the car and pulled over to side of the road.

"What are you doing?" Elvis said as he looked up at his old friend in the mirror. "What's got to be done? And why are you stoppin'? What the hell's goin' on?"

In the mirror, Elvis could see the reflection of two sets of headlights approaching from behind. He heard the squeal of tires and the grinding of the gravel on the side of the road as each vehicle came to a screeching halt, the first directly in front of the limo and the second one sandwiching them in from behind. He watched two men exit the rear doors of the large, black van in the front. He couldn't make sense of what was happening. *Why is Dave just sitting there? We've gotta get out of here*, he thought. As the two men quickly approached his door, he could hear more footsteps crunching through the gravel from behind.

"Lock the doors!" he yelled to Dave. He couldn't believe his friend was making no move to help. He opened up a small compartment hidden under the floor mat and reached for the gun inside. It wasn't there. He quickly pushed down the small lock on the door nearest him. He slid over to the other side of the seat to lock the other, but as his hand was inches away from the lock, the door was pulled open. He could see two large men, dressed in black, blocking his way. He scrambled back over to the other side of the car and braced his back against the door, extended his feet in the direction of the two men and prepared to kick with all his might, but at that moment he heard the click of the lock in the door behind him being released.

"Dave! What are you doing?" he yelled as the door behind him was yanked open and he tumbled halfway out of the car. He was pulled the rest of the way out by two other men who had been waiting for him there. As they dragged him away, he tried to wrench his hands from their grasp. He felt his large ring pulled from his finger during the struggle and heard a faint clink as it struck the pavement.

"Who the hell are you guys? Dave, help me!" he yelled. As he struggled with the two men, he could see out of the corner of his eye that Dave was out of the car and watching with his arms folded, as though he were a foreman overseeing his orders being carried out.

"What's goin' on? Help me Dave!"

The two men restraining Elvis were joined by a third, and together they dragged him toward the van parked behind the limo. Elvis was pinned in from all directions by the three men, and though he realized there was no way out of their grasp, he was determined to give them a good fight. He yanked with all his might and managed to pull his right arm free. He balled up his fist and swung hard, delivering a crushing blow to the face of the man on his left. The man released his grip on Elvis and brought his hands to his own face in an attempt to stem the steady gush of blood coming from his nose. Elvis sensed this might be his last chance at escape and thrust his right leg hard toward the largest of the three men, who was directly in front of him, but as his leg approached his target, the man caught Elvis' foot and pulled it up, causing Elvis to lose his balance and go crashing to the ground in a loud thud. He felt the breath escape his lungs and tried desperately to pull the air back into his chest.

The man with the bloody nose, having recovered his senses, raised his fist over Elvis' face as if ready to deliver a fatal blow, but the largest of the three goons grabbed the man's fist mid-air and yelled, "Stop! He's not to be hurt." Elvis saw the third man raise a syringe over him and felt the long needle pierce his skin, driving deep into the tissue of his forearm. Tape was placed over Elvis' mouth, and then the three men lifted him from the ground, rendering him helpless, with all of his limbs being controlled by these thugs. As he was carried away in the direction of the rear vehicle, he watched as another man reached out for Dave. Elvis thought his friend was now being caught up in the abduction, another victim in whatever plot these evil men were carrying out, but dismissed that thought as he watched his old friend greet the other man as though they were buddies.

Elvis was placed into the back seat of the waiting van, which then pulled in line behind the first van, and the two cars sped away into the night. A short time later, Elvis' struggles subsided, and his head dropped to his chest.

"Hurry up, Coop," Dave said while he gripped the steering wheel of the limo and looked to the man who was entering the passenger side of the car. "We need to get to the Lisa Marie, and quick."

"What?" Coop replied with a start. "The Lisa Marie plane? I thought you meant Elvis' other plane. Damn, he's gonna kill us."

"Just get your ass in the car right now," Dave said. "The clothes are in the back. Change as fast as you can."

As Dave watched the taillights of the two vans disappear down the road in front of him, the struggle he was engaged in continued to torment his thoughts. He could still see the look of betrayal on his friend's face, and he fought back the guilt that was starting to settle down around his heart. He forced his thoughts back to the task at hand.

—

Chapter 9

While Elvis was being taken from the van and carried onto Richard's private jet at a small airstrip in a remote location north of Memphis, Dave pulled into the Memphis International Airport on the southeast side of the city and parked in front of the Lisa Marie plane. Coop emerged from the passenger side of the limousine dressed in Elvis' white sequined jump suit, the one that had become seared into the memories of anyone who had seen his *Elvis: Aloha from Hawaii* special.

The air traffic controller who looked down on the scene from his perch high above was one such person for whom that image of Elvis was indelibly etched into his memory. "Hey, there goes Elvis again. Man, that guy never takes off those clothes," he said, prompting the man next to him to laugh.

As Coop entered the plane, another man emerged and gave Dave a thumbs-up signal. The man slipped into the back seat of the limousine, and Dave checked off another item on his list.

Dave regretted what had to be done as he watched the Corvair 880 taxi away. He watched as the name painted on its side, Lisa Marie, slowly drifted out of view and the letters "TCB," which adorned its tail, blurred from sight.

A short time later, Coop looked down to the cockpit gauge and waited for the altimeter to reach the target number. When it hit 13,000 feet, he set the automatic pilot and got up from his seat. He entered the main cabin and approached a timer attached to a bundle of explosives. He clicked the small red button at its center and watched as the digital clock on the mechanism began to count down. He looked around the empty plane and admired the lavish styling throughout and thought, *What a damn shame. Elvis is definitely gonna kill us.* He strapped on a parachute, opened the latch to the side door, and jumped.

He held his hands close to his sides and pointed his head toward the ground so he could reach maximum velocity and put as much distance between him and the plane as possible. By the light of the moon, he could see the landscape below him start to take shape, growing closer and larger as he sped toward the ground, and he could hear the deafening sound of the wind as it rushed past his ears. At the last possible second, he pulled the cord, and the parachute unfurled behind him, pulling him up sharply. He grabbed the strings that attached the chute to the pack strapped around his shoulders and enjoyed the gentle descent. At this speed, he could barely hear the wind as it gently whistled past his ears. A few moments later, he heard a huge explosion and turned around to see the Lisa Marie exploding into the night, sending out several waves of flames and sparks into the star-filled sky above.

Chapter 10

Spanish moss trailed from the branches of the tall oak trees lining either side of the long driveway, and a lazy night breeze blew the moss gently in the direction of the large mansion in the distance, beckoning Dave to move forward and finish what he had started. He pulled around the large, semi-circular driveway in front of the mansion, and as he exited the car he marveled at the sight of the immense estate. He could hear Richard's voice calling to him from above.

"Come on up, the door's open."

Dave looked to the veranda above and saw Richard motioning for him to come up. He could see the faint red glow of the Cuban cigar Richard held in his hand and caught its strong scent drifting down in his direction, carried by the gentle breeze.

As Dave opened the ornately carved door gracing the front of the home, he couldn't help but compare the mansion to Graceland. Though this enormous structure far eclipsed the more modest estate, he much preferred the more intimate feeling that Graceland provided and couldn't understand how Richard could continue to live behind these walls with no one to keep him company. He pitied the younger man for his solitary life.

As he climbed toward the second floor, he admired the design of the huge double staircase that gently wound its way up to the landing. He couldn't help but laugh that the young man was stuck with the muted pink tones of the marble that lined the floors, a design choice made by the man's mother, who chose it because she was trying to stick with the theme of the pink Georgian marble that graced the façade of the mansion. Dave navigated the second floor and eventually made his way out to the veranda and joined Richard.

"Damn, took me thirty minutes to get up here."

"Have a cigar," Richard offered.

Dave took the cigar and sat next to Richard at a small table, where he helped himself to a glass of the whiskey sitting in front of him.

"Before I tell ya what happened, I've been wantin' to ask you this question. This is the biggest home I've ever seen in my life. Why don't you sell it and get yourself a penthouse in the city so you can just walk to work?"

"The only family I ever knew died in that car crash, and this is the only personal connection I have to them. I still feel them here with me. This is where I'm gonna live, and this is where I'm gonna die."

"Yeah, I get it. I understand. I miss them too." Dave shook his head slowly, feeling Richard's sadness.

"Well, how'd it go?" Richard asked.

"Elvis freaked out. He even popped one of my guys in the nose."

"He did?" Richard said with a laugh. "That's so cool. Captain Marvel would have been proud."

"Except for him getting in a few good licks, everything else went like clockwork. He should be arriving at the island in a few hours. The Lisa Marie..." Dave paused to look at his watch, which now read 3:14 a.m., "just blew up 15 minutes ago. I told Coop I'd call him about now."

"When are you leaving for the island?" Dave asked.

"I'll be there in a few days, but you? Well, we'll just have to figure that out when the time's right."

"Ya know, this is the hardest thing I've ever done in my life," Dave said. "What he's gonna go through is beyond me, not to mention what's coming down the road."

"You know we have top-notch physicians and nurses that specialize in detox and therapy on staff, and when he's ready for the trainers, these guys are the best of the best," Richard said.

"Yeah, I know that," Dave said as he stood up and leaned against the railing of the veranda and looked down onto the front gardens and out to the large horse pasture beyond. "It's just hard for me. I hope he doesn't hate me for what I did."

"You mean for what we both did," Richard said. "And how could you blame him? He'll hate both of us, but he'll get over it in time."

"I'm getting drunk," Dave said as he poured himself another drink. "Can I crash here?"

"Of course you can."

"I'm gonna call Coop first," Dave said. "I'll let ya know what's happenin'."

After Dave left the veranda, Richard was left alone with his thoughts. The moonlight danced along the blades of grass in the distant pasture, and the light breeze flowed across its surface, resembling the gentle waves of a calm sea. Richard allowed himself a few minutes to soak in the soothing sight, but as every sea captain knows, there is often a quiet calm before a storm, and

Richard knew he had to brace himself for the on-slaught to come. He pulled another long puff of his cigar, looked up toward the night sky, and allowed his thoughts to drift into the past once again.

Chapter 11

Richard recalled a day from the summer of '67. He was home from school, enjoying the long break between his sophomore and junior year of college. He spent most days at the office with his father learning the family business, but his nights and weekends were his own, and he took full advantage of the new freedoms that came along with the twenty-first birthday he had recently celebrated. He spent many a late night that summer enjoying the company of his friends and soaking up the bluesy soul of Memphis.

He had just gotten home after spending the afternoon hanging out with a group of friends at a local watering hole. He opened the door in a rush and was looking forward to telling his parents about his day. The house may have been expansive from the outside, but when he and his parents were within its walls together, it was simply their home.

"Dad? Mom? You here?" he called out.

"We're in the living room." He heard his mother's voice reply. "Can you come here for a minute?" It was then he noticed the strange pitch in her voice and sensed she was upset. Richard walked into the living room and instantly knew something was wrong. He could see the somber look of his father and watched as his mother covered her face to hide her tears.

"What's wrong?" Richard asked, staring deep into his father's eyes, as if trying to pull the answer from within their depths. "Who died?"

"Your number came up today, son," his father said. Richard could feel the heaviness of his father's heart as he delivered those words, the words that hung in the air for many long seconds while Richard absorbed their meaning.

"My number?" he asked, and then answered his own question. "I've been drafted."

"I'll stop this. I know who to call," his dad said with the air of authority that usually had a steadying effect on Richard. But today he would find no solace in the words as he forced himself to stand at odds with his father.

"You're kidding, right? No way will I let you get me out of this. I'm no better than anybody else," Richard said, thinking of several of his close friends who had already been called up to serve. He then stood up a bit taller and said with a firm resolve, "When and where do I go?"

He heard his mother's tears grow louder. Not able to look in her direction, he continued to look toward his father, who pulled him close and said, "I'm proud of you, son."

* * * *

Not long after Richard started his stint in the South Vietnamese jungle, he met Coop. He had been shooting the breeze with a few of the guys from his platoon. The sound of the Stones could be heard coming through the radio in the tent nearby, and he could smell the overpowering scent of the joint which a few of the men in his unit were passing back and forth to each other. He pulled out one of the magazines he'd brought with him from the States, hoping to avoid the awkward moment he knew was coming, the moment they would pass the joint in his direction and he would decline, becoming the butt of yet another one of their jokes. The magazine had a picture of Elvis on the cover and the title story "*Elvis in the Army.*" As he began to read the stale articles within its pages, he was rudely interrupted by one of the men in his unit.

"Elvis in the Army?" the other man said, flicking the magazine cover. "That was ages ago. That guy's a has-been."

"Hey guys, we've got a Presley fan here," he taunted. He started throwing around a couple of Richard's other magazines, which all had pictures of Elvis on their covers.

The other men in the group joined in, laughing at Richard and mimicking Elvis. They swiveled their hips, swung their arms wildly, held up make-believe microphones, and butchered the lyrics to "Heartbreak Hotel." Richard silently endured the ribbing, knowing if he protested it would only rile them up further. He was resolved to ride out the embarrassing moment and secretly tuck the magazines away, but then he noticed a large man coming in their direction. *Oh great*, he thought, *another jerk coming to join in the fun. Can this get any worse?* But Richard was surprised to find he had an ally when the man said, "Back off, guys. Next asshole who makes fun of Elvis is gonna be thrown off my chopper. I'll leave you behind and let the Viet Cong skin you alive."

Take that, you assholes, Richard thought as he watched the group disband and slink away.

"Hey buddy. I'm Joel, but you can call me Coop," the man introduced himself. "Looks like you were all shook up."

Richard and Coop both laughed at the Elvis reference.

"Thanks. I'm Richard, and those guys ain't nothin' but hound dogs."

What was to be a great friendship started to grow as they both laughed and shook hands in that sticky jungle halfway across the world from Memphis, which they later learned was the city they both called home.

* * * *

After eighteen long months of service to his country, Richard was headed back home. Along with several other men in his unit, he boarded the military aircraft for the long flight back to the States. He had actually grown close to the men over the many long months they had spent in the jungle. He no longer felt apart from the group, but had instead earned their respect as he fought beside them, laughed beside them, and cried beside them during those quiet times they all mourned for those among their ranks who had fallen.

After twenty-four hours on the long military flight, Richard watched the rugged coast of Northern California as it slowly took shape along the horizon far into the distance, beyond the great Pacific Ocean being pulled upon its shores. The pilot banked left and travelled north up the shore for several miles, and Richard soaked in the sight of the majestic California coastline while the early morning sun sent slivers of light through wispy patches of clouds that hung along the coast. The two tall towers of the Golden Gate Bridge came into view, and the thin layer of fog that shrouded their base made them appear to be floating above the choppy waters of the San Francisco Bay. The pilot banked right and headed over the bridge, flying at an angle over its center span, and that's when Richard spotted Alcatraz Island in the center of the bay to his right. He thought about the penitentiary housed on that small island and couldn't help but compare it to the hellhole from which he had just been liberated.

A short while later, their flight landed at the Travis Air Force Base. Richard gathered his pack and headed down the stairs, prepared to board another long flight to Memphis. He paused midway down the steps to savor the moment. *Back in the good old US of A*, he thought while he breathed in the crisp morning air. It was at that moment he imagined he heard his mother's voice calling to him, "Richard! Richard! Over here!" As he turned in the direction of the voice, he realized it was, indeed, his mother; she and his father were both waving up at him.

Unable to contain his excitement, Richard hurried down the last few steps and ran to meet his mother, who was running in his direction. He threw his bag down, and they wrapped their arms around each other. She pulled back, grabbed his face in her hands, and stared at him for a long moment.

"We're so proud of you, son. Look at you...you're not our little boy anymore. Thank God you made it back to us," she said. Richard's father joined them, and the three of them enjoyed a long embrace. Richard thought back to another excited embrace they shared many years ago, and he too thanked the Lord that he was once again safely by their side.

By this time, Coop had exited the plane and was standing back to give his friend a moment alone with his parents. Richard noticed him standing nearby and motioned him over.

"Thanks for everything, Coop," Richard said, and then introduced his friend to his parents. He had mentioned Coop often in the letters he'd written home to them, so he was glad to finally have a chance to introduce them.

"Hey man, I'll call you soon," Richard said to Coop as they parted ways.

"Get outta here," Coop said. "Memphis awaits your return."

Coop stood with a group of men from Richard's unit, and they all watched as Richard walked arm in arm between his parents and approached a nearby jet with the moniker *Hart of Memphis* emblazoned on its side.

"Who the hell is that guy?" one of the men asked.

"Well assholes," Coop said and then paused for effect. "Let's just say he's flying home on his own jet."

"Shit, we spent the last year with Richie Rich," one of the men said to the rest of the group, who stood with their mouths agape.

"You have no idea, ass wipes," Coop said.

"Hey Coop, you want to catch a ride?" he heard Richard call out from across the tarmac.

"Hell yeah," he called back, and then to his companions he jokingly teased, "See ya, lowlifes."

It was on that flight back to Memphis that Coop warmed his way into the hearts of Richard's parents and eventually took over as the family's private pilot a few years later.

Chapter 12

Having indulged himself long enough in memories from his past, Richard took one last puff of his cigar, exhaled slowly, snuffed it out in the ashtray, and pulled his thoughts once again to the present. He was anxious to hear if his friend Coop had completed the task and was out of harm's way, so he headed downstairs to listen in on Dave's call.

As Richard walked into the living room below, Dave was speaking excitedly into the phone. "Hey Coop, glad you're home. So how'd it go? And don't leave anything out...Fantastic...Oh, and remember, keep that low profile we talked about. The longer everyone thinks you died with Elvis, the easier it will be to keep this secret. Be sure to let me know anything that could compromise this operation. Thanks, and I'll talk to ya soon."

Richard felt a surge of relief as he listened to the conversation, knowing his friend was out of harm's way.

"Just like we planned," Dave said to Richard.

"Go get some sleep, and I'll get you up in a few hours," Richard said. "By then the world should be finding out that the King of Rock 'n' Roll is dead."

* * * *

Later that morning, Dave and Richard sat on the sofa in the living room at the Hart Estate and watched as Walter Cronkite delivered a breaking news report.

"It was just learned that Elvis Presley, known as the King of Rock 'n' Roll and the most famous entertainer in the world, is missing and presumed dead after his plane exploded mid-flight. As we have it now, the only people killed were Mr. Presley and his private pilot, Joel Cooper. News is coming in rapidly, and we will keep you up to date on this tragic event. The world is in shock and in mourning. Please stay with us for further developments."

"This is really happening," Dave said as he pulled his attention away from the screen and looked toward Richard. "I better get to

Graceland to be with the family. I'll call you later."

Richard stared at Dave for a long moment and then said, "Damn, here we go."

Chapter 13

Still sleeping off the aftereffects of the previous night, Lane Bishop lay passed out on the sofa wearing the same clothes he had put on the day before. An empty bottle of Jack Daniels sat on the floor next to him, and beside it was an ashtray filled with cigarette butts. A phone could be heard ringing incessantly, but Lane did not wake until he heard a banging on the wall and an angry neighbor yelling, "Answer the damn phone!"

Lane opened one eye slowly, just a crack, and cringed as the bright light from the late morning sun assaulted his senses. He looked at the clock on the bookshelf across the room, and the numbers 11:21 on the digital display slowly came into focus. The loud ringing of the phone pierced his consciousness, and he reached toward the side table next to him, knocked the receiver to the floor with a loud bang, fumbled around to retrieve it, and eventually managed to place it next to his ear.

"Yeah," he mumbled into the phone.

"Where the hell are you?" he heard the angry voice of a man on the other end.

"What? Who is this?" Lane said and forced himself to sit up. He shook his head in an attempt to clear the fog within, but unfortunately for him, it set off a throbbing between his temples which became worse as the voice on the other side of the line screamed even louder.

"This is your boss, asshole. Where the hell are you? You should have been here the minute you heard."

"Heard what?"

"Heard what? You livin' under a damn rock? Get your ass to Graceland right now."

"For what? What the hell you talkin' about?"

"Elvis is dead. Elvis is dead. I should fire your ass. Get to Graceland."

Lane winced and pulled the phone away from his ear. "Oh shit!" he exclaimed and jumped up.

He decided there was no time to change out of his rumpled clothes, so he grabbed the jacket he had pulled off the night before, hoping it would mask their appearance. He grabbed the pack of cigarettes from the coffee table, put one in his mouth, grabbed a notepad, and rushed out the door.

As he approached the gates of Graceland a few minutes later, he hurriedly patted down his hair and rubbed the stubble on his face, regretting his decision to leave in such a rush. He had no idea there would be so many people here. A large crowd was gathered at the gates, and their numbers were increasing by the minute. He watched as some of them placed flowers on the ground, lighted candles, and set up makeshift memorials to Elvis. Throngs of people were gathered at the gates crying, holding hands, hugging, and visibly shaken. He got out of his car with notepad and pen in hand and joined the ranks of the other reporters and news crews who were interviewing the inconsolable Elvis fans all around them. It seemed very surreal to Lane until he heard a nearby news reporter broadcasting live. Upon hearing her words, the reality of the day started to sink in.

"It is confirmed; Elvis Aaron Presley, 42, was killed…"

* * * *

Several hundred miles away in Nashville, Johnny Cash sat with his guitar in his hand, a pencil in his mouth, and a piece of sheet music in front of him. He stared at the television and heard that very same reporter deliver the news, "...at approximately one o'clock this morning, Elvis Presley's plane, the Lisa Marie, had a mid-air explosion. No word yet on the cause of the accident. Killed in the explosion were Elvis Presley and his pilot, Joel Cooper. Mr. Presley is survived by his only child, Lisa Marie, 9, and his father, Vernon Presley, 61."

"And the earthquake begins," Johnny said to himself as a sly grin came to his face. "Good luck, E."

Chapter 14

A small plane touched down on a private island somewhere in the Caribbean. Elvis was removed from the plane by two men dressed in
hospital scrubs. They placed Elvis, who was still
unconscious, on a stretcher and loaded him into
the back of a large, white van. He was then
driven away from the airstrip and down a dark,
narrow road that wound through a thick tropical
jungle. The road led past a home that jutted out
of the hillside overlooking the ocean and eventually led out of the shadows of the jungle into the
brightly lit area below. To the right of the road
was a large compound, composed of several
buildings. To the left of the road was a wide expanse of land which was bordered by more of the
thick jungle, and beyond the compound, a beach
stretched out in both directions.

The vehicle turned right toward the compound, passed under the large arch which

marked the entry to the area, and stopped in front of a large building. Elvis was wheeled inside its walls and was taken to a small room where he was transferred from the stretcher onto a bed which had been bolted to the floor. Restraints were placed on his arms and legs, and an IV was inserted into the radial vein of his right arm. The lights were dimmed, and he was left alone to sleep off the aftereffects of the strong sedative which had been administered during his abduction. At the nurse's station across the hall, a nurse watched the live video feed being transmitted from the small room and noted all the details in a chart on the desk in front of her.

In a nearby office, Dr. Colby was reflecting on a conversation he'd had with Richard Hart a few days prior when Richard and Dave Carson had come to the island.

* * * *

"Doc, how soon after he arrives do you think I'll be able to talk to him?" Richard had asked.

"Well, this is how it's going to play out," he had replied. "His hell will start within 24 hours and then most likely peak within 48 to 72 hours. His condition will continue to get worse before it gets better. You can probably talk to him within a few days of his arrival. I'll let you know. We will have him monitored 24 hours a day."

"We got you here and paid you well," Richard had said, "because you're the best. Do whatever you have to do. Just get him clean."

"Look Richard, I can get him physically clean in two to three weeks, and then I'll start the training regimen. But he's going to need a lot of therapy and counseling for months on end."

"Therapists, counselors, we've got the best of those, too," Richard had told him. "They'll be here in a few days. I would like to know his status every four hours after he arrives."

"Yes sir, I got it."

"Hey Doc, can you gather all the staff in the morning? I just want to meet them and introduce myself. Dave and I will be jetting out of here right after that. Can you set that up for me?"

* * * *

Dr. Colby had turned his attention back to the task at hand when the nurse called from the adjoining room, "Sir, he's waking up."

From within the small room, Elvis began to stir. He opened his eyes and looked around at his surroundings. He saw the IV bag that hung from a stand next to his right shoulder, and with his eyes he followed the tube that lead out from the bottom and discovered that it ended where a needle was taped to his forearm. *What the hell?* he thought. *I'm pullin' this thing out.* He lifted his left arm, planning to reach over and yank out the IV, but there was a resistance that prevented him from lifting it any higher than a few inches. He looked at his wrist and saw that a heavy leather strap had been wound around it and attached to the bed. He found another had been wrapped around his right wrist and two more around each of his ankles. *Oh my God, oh my God. I've got to get out of here.*

"Where the hell am I?" he yelled out as he struggled wildly with his restraints. He yanked each arm with all his might but couldn't break free, so he jerked them up and down hoping he could weaken whatever mechanism was keeping them fastened to the bed. He tried to kick his legs up and from side to side, but in all directions he had but two or three inches of slack. Try as he might, his struggles made not a single bit of difference.

"Why am I tied up? What's going on? Untie me now!" he yelled out from the empty confines of the room which was now his prison.

From the corner of his eye, he caught a movement on the right side of the room and jerked his head sharply in its direction. He watched as a short, portly man entered the room. He wore a white lab coat and glasses with thick, black frames. Elvis felt like a caged animal in the zoo as the man studied him from head to toe in a detached, clinical manner while jotting down notes on a clipboard in clipped, rapid strokes of his pen. *What kind of maniacal experiment have I been forced into?*

"Mr. Presley," the man said very calmly as he peered at Elvis over the top of his glasses. "My name is Dr. Colby. I'm here to help you. I'm in charge of your recovery."

"In charge of what? Recovery? Let me loose!" Elvis screamed at the man. "My friends, family, the police will be looking for me. Do you know who I am, you idiot? "

"Who you are is why you're here," the man said in a relaxed voice. "That's all I can say about it. The person who will explain everything to you, including why no one is looking for you, will be here in a few days. And to be honest, Mr. Presley, you have no say-so in this matter. I'm going to do my job now and try to stop this from being the worst day of your life."

"Well that's impossible, because it already is."

Chapter 15

Nausea overcame Elvis in the early evening during that first day on the island. He began to sweat profusely, his stomach clenched involuntarily, and he could feel the bile start to rise. His hands were still fastened tightly at his sides, so he lifted his right shoulder and leaned as far over to his left side as possible in an attempt to prevent the contents of his stomach from erupting all over his chest. As the first wave of sickness hit, a basin appeared in front of him, held out by a nurse who had silently slipped into the room. He retched into the kidney shaped bowl and let out a loud moan right before the second wave hit and he puked up what felt like his entire stomach. When his insides began to calm, he leaned back on the pillow and closed his eyes. He felt a cool, moist towel being laid on his brow and felt a deep gratitude to the nurse at his side for just a moment before the reality of the situation sank in again, and then he despised her for the part she was playing in his torment.

A male nurse entered the room to take Elvis' vital signs. He placed the cuff around Elvis' upper arm and pumped the attached bulb, which caused the cuff to constrict tightly around his arm. Elvis could feel the blood pulsate beneath the cuff and watched as the nurse placed a stethoscope on the inside crease of his elbow.

The female nurse held up a glass of water to Elvis as well as a small white paper cup which contained four pills of varying sizes and colors.

"I ain't takin' that shit, bitch," Elvis lashed out at her, and turning to the male nurse, he said, "And you, don't you dare touch me. Who the hell are you anyway?"

"Bitch? Son, didn't your mama teach you to respect your elders?" the female nurse said. "I've got a name; it's Joyce."

"Don't bring my mama into this!"

"Okay, if you want to keep on having all your pain and throwing up and feeling like you're about to die," Joyce said while withdrawing the water and medication, "that's fine with me."

The male nurse removed the blood pressure cuff from around Elvis' arm, and put away his stethoscope. He motioned to the female nurse, and together they headed toward the door.

"Okay, okay, if it's gonna make me feel better, do whatever you have to do. Just get it done and do it quick and get the hell outta here. What are you givin' me?"

"Something to help get you through what you're going through," Joyce said as she placed the pills in his mouth and offered him a drink to wash them down. "It's methadone. It will help you with the cravings and your pain, and valium and clonidine for your muscle cramps and to help stabilize your vital signs. We'll dispense these medications every six hours for the next few days."

Lord, what is happenin' to me, his thoughts cried up to heaven.

Chapter 16

Early in the afternoon on the third day of captivity, Elvis was still strapped to the bed in the small room which had become his prison cell. His body was still rebelling at the sudden withdrawal of the substances it had become addicted to over the many years during which Elvis had indulged his cravings. Every inch of his body was painful to the touch. He felt the hair on the back of his arms standing up as though a chill were upon him, but there was also sweat dripping from his forehead, and a fire burned from within. He grimaced in pain as another round of tremors overtook him. He wanted to curl up in a ball, but the restraints still prevented his movements. Over the past few days, he had been untied from the bed every few hours while a couple of the male attendants escorted him across the hall to the restroom. He had also been unstrapped from his restraints one other time: they had to change his clothes and the bed sheets to remove the strong scent of the urine that his body had involuntarily released, leaving him feeling helpless and humiliated.

It was on this day that Richard arrived on the island. As he walked into the small room, he braced himself for the onslaught he knew Elvis would unleash upon him.

"Who the hell are you?" Elvis hissed. "Another jerk thinking I need help?"

"Mr. Presley, you really believe you don't need help?" Richard asked while he steadied himself and did his best to assume the air of authority he knew his dad would have exuded at this moment. But as he looked at his idol staring at up at him, he could feel the hatred burning behind the man's steely blue eyes, and it hurt him to be the object of the man's contempt. "Let me see, for the last twenty years, you were on amphetamines, sedatives, barbiturates, narcotics, and you've overdosed twice in the last year. You checked yourself into the hospital telling people it was exhaustion. You want me to go on?"

"I said who the hell are you, and how do you know so much about me? "

"I'm Richard Hart," he said while grabbing a chair and sitting a few feet from Elvis' side. He studied Elvis' reaction, wondering if the man would recognize his name, but did not detect even the slightest recognition. "I'm the guy who kidnapped and brought you to this island to save your life."

"Save my life? It's your life I'd be worried about when I get loose."

"Really? I'll take that into consideration."

"Richard Hart?" Elvis said and paused for a moment. Richard was afraid that Elvis had recognized his name, but the moment of worry passed when Elvis continued. "And what did that Dr. Colby mean when he said no one is looking for me? What about the Colonel?"

"I took care of the Colonel. I gave him enough cash that he's probably drowning in it right now."

"So I take it money was no object to pull this bullshit you did on me."

"You're dead, Mr. Presley," Richard said as he stood up and looked down at Elvis. "You're dead to your fans, the world, even your family. To them, you blew up in the Lisa Marie last week when I faked your death."

"You blew up my plane? The world thinks I'm dead? My dad, my little girl think I'm dead?" Elvis screamed out in a rage. "Dead is what you're going to be when I get out of here!"

"You didn't have much time to live," Richard said calmly as he sat back down. "You're lucky you didn't die from your overdoses. I did what I did to save you."

Richard thought of his father and wondered how his dad and Dave had conceived of this crazy plan. Never in his wildest imagination did he ever think he'd be holding Elvis Presley prisoner on a remote island. *This is insane*, he thought.

"Save me? I already told you, I don't need savin', are you deaf?"

As Richard started to rise, Elvis yelled out, "Okay, okay, just explain what's going on and when I'm getting out of here."

"After you're clean, trained, and looking like the bad-ass Elvis that everybody loved, that's when. You have a long, very hard road in front of you. I have brought together the best doctors, trainers, therapists, and dietitians in the world to get you in shape both physically and mentally."

As Richard got up to leave the room, Elvis demanded, "I'll ask you one more time, when am I gettin' outta here?"

"When I think you're ready, that's when. I'll be back tomorrow."

"Don't leave! I need more answers. Please don't leave. Who are you?"

"I'll have more answers for you tomorrow," Richard calmly replied, and then he exited the room.

Chapter 17

On day four of Elvis' detox, Richard once again entered the small room where Elvis was being confined. Elvis continued to feel the same withdrawal symptoms as the previous day, but he felt more lucid. If looks could kill, the daggers he sent in Richard's direction would most certainly have proven fatal. He despised the young man who held him hostage, and he'd be damned if he would just give in without a fight.

"How you feeling today?" Richard asked.

"Just fantastic, never felt better. I'm ready for a marathon, dickhead," Elvis snapped. "How 'bout releasing my arms and legs? You even have your muscle guys take me to the bathroom watching me take a crap. How stupid is that?"

"I'm here to answer some of your questions, then I'm leaving for a month," Richard said as he folded his arms in front of himself as if to deflect the fiery wrath being sent his way from across the room. "I have to get back to Memphis. I have things I need to do."

"*Some* of my questions? No, you're gonna answer *all* my questions," Elvis demanded.

"I only have a few minutes, so take a second and ask me the ones you need answered most. My staff has been directed to help you in every way to help in your recovery, but they've also been directed to not answer any questions that have to do with the end game."

"End game? Okay, there's my first question. What the hell is the end game?"

"I'll get right to it then. This is what's going to happen. Starting next week in every major market in the world, on every major network and radio station and in every newspaper, every single day until May 24th of next year, I will be promoting an extraordinary event that will happen on that day."

"That's gonna cost you a pretty penny."

"Tell me about it."

"And what the hell happens on May 24th, pray tell, besides being Priscilla's birthday?"

"You're the May 24th, Mr. Presley," Richard said and pointed at Elvis. "We're shocking the world on that day."

"Shocking the world?" Elvis asked. "What are you talkin' about? Am I dead? Am I in hell?"

"I'm trying to get you out of that hell," Richard said.

"What about my little girl?" Elvis asked, and his heart grew heavy at the thought of her, wishing he could dry the tears he knew would most certainly be falling.

"Don't you worry none, you're going to be with her and your dad soon enough," Richard said. "There's someone watching out for them."

"Wouldn't happen to be that asshole Dave, would it?" Elvis asked. It cut him to the core that the last thing he'd seen before losing consciousness on the night of his abduction was the sight of his old friend shaking hands with one of his kidnappers. "I need to talk to you about him. How big a part did he have in this?"

"Time's up," Richard said as he checked his watch. "I've got to go."

Chapter 18

After Richard's visit, Elvis was feeling even more agitated and irritable. Spending four days tied to this bed, surrounded by bare walls with not even a window to gaze through, was almost more than he could endure and not break with reality. He was still suffering the agonizing effects of his withdrawals and wondered why the medicines being administered to him every six hours seemed to be making no difference at all. He wondered if he was being poisoned and resolved to refuse the medications the next time they were offered. He didn't trust that Richard guy any further than he could throw him. He had to figure out how to get out of this place. Surely he wasn't far from Memphis; he was bound to recognize something if he were to make a break for it. He had been formulating an escape plan for a few days, being careful to note every detail of the area between his room and the restroom across the hall. With each trip to the restroom, he was able to memorize another aspect in the layout of the building. He was ready to make a move.

* * * *

His heart beat wildly in his chest as the two attendants unstrapped his arms from the bed. He rubbed his wrists and raised one of them to his face and scratched that spot at the side of his nose that had been itching incessantly for the last few minutes. What a relief it was to be able to move his arms again. He relished these moments before each of the restroom breaks. The mere act of being able to move his arms and legs freely for a few short minutes was the only small pleasure afforded him during the torturous time he had spent locked inside this small room with not even a window to connect him to the outside world.

Elvis walked with the men to the bathroom, where they took guard on either side of the door. He closed the door behind him, relieved they no longer felt the need to accompany him inside the small bathroom as they had during the first few days of his captivity. He looked at his reflection in the small bathroom mirror and barely recognized himself. His eyes were sunk deep into his face and surrounded by dark circles. His sideburns were now joined by a thick layer of whiskers that covered the rest of his face and ran below his chin and extended down his neck. He stared at that face looking back at him and said to himself, "It's showtime. Let's do this thing."

At that moment, he yanked the IV from his arm, jerked open the bathroom door, and quickly ran away from the two startled attendants. He passed the nurses' station, which was currently empty, and ran toward the door at the end of the hall. Between him and the door were two staff members, who had turned when they heard the commotion. They saw Elvis running in their direction and took a stance, ready to tackle him as he approached, but without breaking stride, Elvis pushed them aside and broke free from the confines of the building as he pushed open the door.

The bright sunlight shocked his senses, and he paused a moment to look around and get his bearings. He was amazed to see the brilliant white sand of the dunes in front of him and beyond that, the vast turquoise waters that stretched out for miles into the distance. "That sure as hell doesn't look like the Mississippi to me. Where the hell am I?" He looked to his left and saw a large, flat meadow that stretched for hundreds of yards, disappearing into the jungle beyond. He looked to his right and saw more of the thick jungle, and in that split second he decided the dark cover of that jungle was his best bet at escaping this nightmare.

While Elvis ran into the jungle beyond the door, one of the staff who had been left in his wake behind gathered his senses and began to yell, "Elvis is gone! Hit the alarm!"

"Elvis just left the building," the other staff member said as he pulled himself up from the floor and hit the alarm. "That's just perfect."

Elvis ran deep into the tropical jungle and found himself surrounded by thick growth on all sides. The loud alarm blaring from the compound spurred him on, deeper and deeper into the depths of the jungle. From his left he could see the bright water of the ocean peeking through the dense growth from time to time. There was a thick layer of vegetation on the ground, and he could feel the uneven surface beneath as roots and rocks dug into the tender soles of his bare feet, slowing his progress. He heard a noise behind him and turned quickly in its direction, but his foot lodged between two rocks, and he twisted his ankle and fell to the ground. Three bright green birds with large orange beaks flew out of a bush in front of him. They squawked loudly and flew straight for his face. He covered his head and felt their wings flapping wildly against his hands and their sharp talons digging into his fingers. One of them pecked violently at his head and pulled out several strands of hair. "Ouch!" Elvis yelled as he swung both hands explosively at the birds, causing all three to quickly fly away, disappearing into the canopy of tall palm trees above.

Elvis sat on the ground rubbing his ankle and the back of his hands, which had been scratched and pecked by the birds. His head hurt, his feet were throbbing, he could scarcely catch his breath, and he felt as though his heart were going to burst.

In the distance he could hear loud voices coming from the compound. "You two check the jungle over there. And you two run down to the beach," he could hear commands being belted out. "And go get the pilot. The chopper needs to get up in the air, pronto!"

Elvis thought he heard footsteps approaching and noticed a movement on the ground to his left. A large black rodent darted across his path. "Oh shit!" he yelled, and he jumped up with a start. Aided by the adrenaline that shot through his veins, he ran toward the ocean on his left, hoping he could run along the edge of the jungle and the beach to avoid detection while staying away from the crazy wildlife within the dark shadows of the forest. As he sped toward the open air, his foot became entangled in the thick forest undergrowth and he fell hard, hitting his head forcefully on a large tree root. He passed out.

Chapter 19

Elvis slowly regained consciousness and found himself strapped to the bed again within the tiny confines of the room which had become his own hell on earth. As he opened his eyes, he could see Dr. Colby and Richard looking down at him.

"Well, Mr. Presley, looks like you held up my takeoff for a few hours. At least you got some exercise to go with that massive headache," Richard said. "I've ordered two staff to be with you now at all times. This won't happen again."

"You can't keep me in here!"

"Yes I can," Richard said and walked to the door.

"I'm getting out of here one way or another!"

"No," Richard said as he pointed his finger firmly at Elvis. "You won't."

"You son of a bitch!" Elvis yelled back.

"Talk to you next month," Richard said and then exited the room.

"Get back here! Let me go! I need to get home!" Elvis yelled as the door slowly closed and Richard disappeared from view.

Upon closing the door, Richard leaned back against it, closed his eyes, and sighed. He could still hear Elvis screaming and thought, *What have I gotten myself into?*

Within the room, Elvis spat toward the door, gritted his teeth, and growled, "I'm gonna kill you when I get outta here."

"Listen, Mr. Presley," Dr. Colby said with a raised voice. "I've had it with all your bullshit regarding Richard. I'm not supposed to talk to you about anything but your recovery, but I've had enough of this. Let me educate you on what Mr. Hart has done in just the past few years."

Elvis refused to look at the doctor but heard the man's words all the same.

"He has built over ten hospitals in third-world countries, providing free medical care at all of them," the doctor continued. "Every single member of the staff is on his payroll. He pays for it all; vaccines, transportation to the hospitals, aftercare, clinics. He has saved thousands of lives, and now he's trying to save yours, and for the life of me, I don't know why."

Elvis allowed a small fraction of what the man said to sink in. He wasn't about to change his mind about his captor.

Dr. Colby left the room, and Elvis was once again alone with his thoughts and the agony of the withdrawals that still racked his body. Over the next few days, his body continued to cramp and ache. He slept sporadically and continued to be irritable and agitated and snap at anyone that dared talk to him. There were times he vomited until all that was left were dry heaves. Throughout it all, the staff was calm, having been well trained to anticipate this reaction.

Chapter 20

The large corporate headquarters of Hart Health Industries towered above a slim young woman standing on the sidewalk below. She stared up at the rows upon rows of windows that lined the tall structure and wondered which one of those windows would soon be the one from which she would stare down at the world below. Her name was Atalynn James, and it was her first day on the job. The sun glistened on her long auburn hair as she nervously touched her headband to ensure not a strand was out of place. She pulled the compact out of her purse and double-checked the makeup which lightly framed the bright blue eyes staring back at her. She patted more powder on her nose and across her cheeks, hoping to cover the freckles that dotted her face. She smoothed the lines of her skirt, though there was not a wrinkle to be seen, and took a deep breath.

"I'm ready," she said quietly to herself.

She exhaled slowly and walked through the large revolving door and into the lobby beyond. As she walked toward the reception desk, she could hear the clicking of her high heels echo through the large expanse of the first floor lobby and felt like every head turned in her direction. She walked up to the reception desk and addressed the two guards sitting behind the counter.

"Hi...um..." she stuttered, and then tamped down the butterflies in her stomach and forced herself to say in a clear confident voice, "I'm starting work today."

"Welcome, what's your name?" one of the guards asked.

"Atalynn James," she replied, preparing to spell her first name as she so often had to do, finding most people thought she was saying Adeline or Anna Lynn, but she was pleasantly surprised that the guard quickly found her name on the clipboard in front of him.

"Here you are, Miss James. Here's your temporary badge. They'll make you a permanent one in the next week or so. And you're working in HR. It's on this floor. Go down that hall, make your first right, and you'll see a sign. Press the buzzer. They'll be expecting you."

"Well, thank you," she replied with a slight Southern lilt, turning in the direction he had pointed.

"Now that's a tall drink of water," one of the guards said as they both watched her walk away.

"You're tellin' me," the other guard nodded in agreement.

* * * *

Having survived the nerves of her first day at the office, Atalynn was at her desk bright and early the next day, excited to continue to learn the ropes of her new job. She had spent most of the day before under the capable tutelage of her supervisor, Sally. The woman had made Atalynn feel welcome and had given her a desk next to a window with a view of the large gardens that graced the center of the office complex. She had learned that Mr. Hart Sr., the founder of the company, had constructed the gardens at the insistence of his wife. Atalynn silently thanked the late Mrs. Hart as she gazed at the variety of plants and colorful flowers growing within. There were sidewalks winding through the perfectly tended tropical plants, and from Atalynn's window, she could see the peaceful path a small creek took as it flowed beneath a stone bridge.

The trees on the other side of the creek's bank stretched up toward the glass rooftop above.

"Ms. James," Sally said, pulling Atalynn's attention back to the busy office. "Can you take this to the fourth floor and give it to Mr. Chavez' secretary?"

"Sure," Atalynn replied as she grabbed the stack of papers. As she exited the elevator on the fourth floor, she held the stack of papers in front of her with both hands. At that very moment, one of the company executives, Mr. Edwards, was approaching the elevator holding his own stack of papers. Unseen to either of them, an angel wearing a Memphis Tigers T-shirt took shape behind Mr. Edwards and pushed the man off balance. The angel then swept into the conference room down the hall where Richard Hart was sitting at a long table, reviewing a report he would soon be discussing with his team. The angel blew Richard's report off the table and into the hall.

Mr. Edwards stumbled into Atalynn, and papers flew everywhere, becoming hopelessly intertwined.

"I'm so sorry," Atalynn said as she bent down and started to pick up the papers. "I'm so sorry. I didn't see you."

"Watch where you're going, young lady! You just screwed up two weeks' worth of important work. I should talk to your boss and see what he would say about this. What's your name?"

"Atalynn James."

"Do you know who I am?"

"No, sir. I'm sorry. I just started here yesterday."

"I'm Mr. Edwards. You find my office and give those papers to my secretary. And watch your step, Miss Clumsy."

"Yes, sir. I'm so sorry."

Atalynn, with tears in her eyes, hurriedly picked up the papers and stepped back into the elevator as Mr. Edwards stood by with his arms crossed, shaking his head.

From his vantage point down the hall, Richard had seen the exchange between Mr. Edwards and the young lady. He had been surprised when the report in front of him had suddenly blown off the table and into the hall. As he stepped out of the conference room to retrieve the report, he heard the commotion down the hall and silently watched the events unfold.

After the elevator doors closed, Richard walked up to Mr. Edwards, startling the man.

"Mr. Hart!" Mr. Edwards quickly recovered his senses to greet his boss. "Good morning."

"I saw how you berated that girl," Richard said.

"Berate?" Mr. Edwards said as he feigned a look of shock. "I never did such a thing," he continued with an indignant tone.

"I saw what you did, and I heard what you said," Richard rebuked him. "No one that works for me will talk to another employee like that. Ever. You're calling her to apologize. Right now."

"I can't do that," Mr. Edwards protested.

"Let's see, what did you say to her?" Richard said and then paused a moment for effect; "Do you know who I am?"

Mr. Edwards was embarrassed to hear his words being parroted back at him.

"You either do it, you do it now," Richard said, "or you hit the road."

Downstairs at HR, Atalynn laid the stack of papers on her desk, sat down, and wiped the tears running down her cheek with the back of her hand. She looked out at the courtyard and let out a loud sigh, fearing this would be the end of her short career at Hart Health Industries. *So much for my rise up the corporate ladder*, she thought.

"What's wrong?" a young girl sitting at the desk next to hers asked. She had befriended Atalynn the day before, and they had developed an instant friendship, bonding over their distinctive names. Her name was Lyndell, and when she introduced herself to Atalynn, she had been quick to point out that although her name was spelled with a "d-e-l-l" at the end, the "e" was silent, so it was actually pronounce "Lindl," which rhymed with "spindle." They both laughed at the lifetimes of interesting introductions their mothers had both provided them by giving them such colorful names.

"I'm fired," Atalynn said as she started to separate the papers in front of her into two stacks, careful to lay Mr. Edward's stack in as neat a manner as possible. "I just started here yesterday, and I'm gonna get fired."

"What happened?" Lyndell asked with concern.

"It doesn't matter. I'm gonna get fired, and I waited so long to get this job."

At that moment the phone on her desk rang.

"Yes ma'am," Atalynn said into the receiver. "I'm on my way."

"I didn't know it would be this quick," Atalynn said to Lyndell as she headed toward Sally's office. "Nice knowing ya."

Atalynn took a long look into the gardens beyond her window, wanting to soak in the sight of them one last time before Sally delivered those two words she knew were soon to come: *You're fired*.

"Mr. Edwards is on the phone for you," Sally said when Atalynn walked into her office. "Why would he want to talk to you? Do you know what this is about?"

"It's about something that just happened," Atalynn replied. She slowly placed the receiver to her ear and winced, assuming Mr. Edwards wanted to deliver the bad news himself.

Sally watched with great interest as the girl picked up the phone.

"Yes, Mr. Edwards," she heard Atalynn say softly into the phone. There was a long pause, and Sally watched as the young woman's face changed from great anxiety to a wide-eyed look of shock. "What?" she heard Atalynn say. "It's okay. No really, it's okay. Thanks, Mr. Edwards."

"So tell me," Sally said as soon as Atalynn hung up the phone, unable to contain her curiosity. "What was that all about?"

"You wouldn't believe me if I told you. I'm so confused," Atalynn replied, and then she walked out of the room, shaking her head.

Upstairs in the fourth floor conference room, Mr. Edwards hung up the phone while Richard stood over him.

"Now doesn't that make you feel better?" Richard asked.

"No. Not really."

"Well it does me, and that's all that counts. Don't let that happen again. Now get back to work."

"Yes, sir," Mr. Edwards replied and slunk out of the conference room.

Richard picked up the phone and dialed his secretary. "Julie, there's a new girl in HR that just started yesterday. I think her last name is James. Can you send her a nice bouquet as a welcome gift from Hart Health? Thanks."

Chapter 21

On day sixth of Elvis' confinement, his body had finally started to ease up on its rebellion. He still felt tremors, but they were slight. Two of the male staff came into the room and removed his straps. He thought they were going to escort him across the hall to the restroom, but they turned as if to leave without him.

"What y'all doin'?" Elvis asked.

"Doctor's orders," they answered.

"Well it's about time," Elvis said as he rubbed his wrists.

"Dr. Colby will be here in the next hour or so to talk to you," one of the men told him as they left.

Elvis could scarcely believe he was free to roam around the room at will. He swung his feet over the side of the bed and sat there for a moment, enjoying his newfound freedom. He stared at the door and resigned himself to not attempt any further escapes until he had more information about his surroundings.

* * * *

In the early evening, a nurse rolled a cart into Elvis' room and wheeled it next to his bed. Elvis breathed in the aroma of the chicken and vegetables that lay in front of him, and he salivated at the sight of the first solid foods he'd been allowed since his stay on the island had begun. The meal set before him was simply a single piece of roasted chicken breast, a small side of steamed green beans, and a few slices of tomato, but to Elvis it seemed like a feast, and he savored each bite.

When he was midway through the meal, Dr. Colby walked into the room. The doctor studied Elvis' appearance, took his pulse, and listened to the strength of his lungs as he held a stethoscope to Elvis' back and asked him to take a deep breath and exhale slowly. The doctor grabbed his reading glasses from the front pocket of his lab coat and jotted down some notes on his clipboard.

"You know," Elvis said to the doctor, "I hate to admit it, but this food ain't so bad."

"I'll let the dietitian know, she'll be glad to hear it," the doctor said, and he looked at Elvis over the top of his glasses. "Now let me give you an update. It's been six days since you got here. Your blood pressure and heart rate are where they need to be. The methadone has helped with your withdrawals. Am I right?"

"Well yeah, I guess. I don't feel nothin' like I did when I came in here. I'm scared to ask this, but what's next?"

"It's almost time to take you to the next level. Our first priority was your physical status, to make sure you didn't die on us. And we've done that," the doctor said, removing the reading glasses and tucking them back into his pocket. "I'm going to keep you here for another few days to monitor you, and then if everything goes okay, we'll move you to a much more comfortable room, and your counseling sessions will begin. One of my staff will come in twice a day to assess your physical status and to continue your medicine. Any questions?"

"Yeah, I got one. Why do I need some shrink to talk to?"

"Let him tell you why, Mr. Presley. You're going to have cravings for the rest of your life. You just can't abuse the drugs that you did for twenty years and think you can lick it in this short while. You do understand that, don't you?"

"I ain't stupid."

"I'll see you soon," the doctor said. He pulled his glasses back out of his pocket, positioned them on the bridge of his nose, looked down at his clipboard, and wrote a few more notes on his way out the door.

Chapter 22

On day ten of Elvis' stay on the island, Dr. Colby led him to his new room. Though Elvis had lived within the spacious walls of the Graceland mansion for years, this new, modest room felt like a palace after the ten days he had just spent locked within the tiny walls of what he had come to refer to as his "detox dungeon." This new room had a large, plush bed and a window on the wall beside it with a view of the beach. As he looked around the room, his eyes came back to that window and focused not on the beautiful scenery beyond, but on the bars that lined the window.

"Y'all still think I can escape this place?" he said. "I don't know where the hell I'm at. I ain't got no transportation. I can't get ahold of nobody. So it's kinda stupid you puttin' bars on the window."

"You can talk to Mr. Hart about that when he gets here," the doctor replied.

"And when is he gonna be here?" Elvis asked. "I need to talk to that guy."

"At this point, I have no idea. I think maybe two or three weeks."

"So what's next, Doc?" Elvis said while shaking his head in disgust at the thought of Richard.

"You know what's next. Your therapy."

"Therapist? Perfect. Those guys try to analyze all the bullshit in your life, then they'll gut you like a catfish. Just what I need. Lookin' forward to it."

"Just to let you know, we have two staff outside the door at all times."

"Of course you do. Like I said, I ain't stupid."

While Dr. Colby walked out of the room, Elvis continued to look around his new surroundings. He saw a sofa and a couple of chairs positioned around a small coffee table. He walked over to a bookshelf, pulled out a few books, and looked forward to immersing himself within the other worlds beyond their covers. But then on the bottom shelf of the bookcase, he spotted a stack of Captain Marvel comic books with a small note attached that read: "Compliments of Richard Hart." *Maybe that guy ain't so bad after all*, he thought. *I wonder how he knew I'd want these.* He pulled one of the comics from the stack and plopped himself down on the sofa to amuse himself with the adventures of the comic book hero who had years ago magically transported young Elvis to another world far from the shadow of the great depression that hung over his childhood home of Tupelo, Mississippi.

* * * *

A few hours later, Elvis stood at the window in his new room and breathed in the fresh scent of the ocean, enjoying the feel of the morning sun on his face. He was interrupted by a knock on the door. He expected that the knock was a simple courtesy being afforded him by the person on the other side who would undoubtedly open the door and let themselves in at any second. But another, more persistent knock followed the first a few seconds later. Elvis got up and opened the door. Standing on the other side was a tall, light-skinned black man. The man's face was clean shaven, and his hair was cut close to his head. He was dressed in a lab coat, much like Dr. Colby's, but this man's had the appearance of a tailored suit. The man's eyes smiled at Elvis, though he did not crack a smile. His skin was clear and youthful, but the crinkles beside his eyes betrayed his age, and Elvis estimated him to be several years his senior.

"Good afternoon Mr. Presley, my name is Dr. Jessup."

"So you're the guy who's gonna tell me how screwed up I am," Elvis said, motioning the man forward toward the sitting area. "Come on in, sit down. I don't think I'm that screwed up, so I don't know why you're here," Elvis said while he sat on the sofa across from the chair that the doctor had chosen. "So let's get to it."

"I have no idea if I can help you," the doctor began. "I have no idea if you can be helped, but I'll promise you this: I'll know something by the end of our session today. I'll know if I can help you or not."

"And what if I don't need help?" Elvis asked.

"Really?" the doctor said in disbelief.

"Okay, okay," Elvis said. "Let's start with this brainwashing."

"In sixty seconds, tell me all about your life," the doctor said.

"Say what? One minute? Are you joking?"

"I don't joke, and I'm waiting."

Elvis looked perplexed, shrugged his shoulders, and began. "I'm 42. I sing for a livin'. I loved my mother. I love my father and my little girl, Lisa Marie. I have regrets like everyone else does, but it's nothing that affects the way I live. I know you all think I have a drug problem. Let me make this clear: I don't smoke pot or snort coke, and I only drink alcohol on rare occasions. I only take prescribed medications from Dr.

Nick, so I don't think I have a problem. That's it. I'm done," he said as he looked at his watch. "Forty-five seconds."

"Can you go twenty-four hours without taking any kind of *medications*?" the doctor asked sarcastically.

"Well, yeah," Elvis snapped back.

"So what I've read here in this report from the last two weeks and this other report about your daily life that Mr. Hart has kept track of since the early '60s are just full of lies? Is that what you're saying?"

"You've got to be kidding," Elvis said. "You've got something there in front of you tellin' you about how I lived inside of Graceland for the past two decades?"

"No. I have a report here that tells me *everything* about your life, inside, outside, wherever you've been, for the past two decades."

"That asshole," Elvis said, shaking his head.

"Who are you talking about?" the doctor asked.

"My ex-best friend, Dave Carson. Just wait till I get my hands on him."

Dr. Jessup looked up from his notes and stared directly at Elvis. "I need you to answer one question and be as honest as you can be. Let's say your mother is asking you this question."

"My mother? Leave her out of all this."

"Believe it or not, Mr. Presley, she's why you're here."

"What's that supposed to mean? I told you once already, you keep my mother out of this. You bring her up one more time, and I'm shutting up, and you can get the hell outta here."

"Okay then," the doctor said, and he started to stand.

"Whoa, whoa, hold on, hold on now," Elvis said while holding his hands up to try to settle the man back into his chair. "So I take it if I don't answer your questions, I ain't never gettin' outta here."

"That's not for me to make that decision. That's up to Mr. Hart."

"Alright, sit down, Doc," Elvis said, and then he settled himself into the cushions of the sofa, folded his arms, and prepared for the conversation to come. "Go ahead. Shoot."

"Okay," the doctor said as he sat back in the chair. "This is your mother asking this question. Son, look into my eyes."

Elvis refused to look at the man's eyes, not wanting to provide him and this absurd question any more credence than he had already done by asking the man to stay.

"Mr. Presley, look at me when I'm talking to you." the doctor scolded him. "I'm going to say this one more time, and if you don't cooperate, I'm walking out."

Elvis begrudgingly looked at the man, knowing his only hope at getting off this god-forsaken island was to pretend to cooperate and wait for the right opportunity to present itself.

"Son, look into my eyes; you've never lied to me before. Are you dying? Are you dying because you can't get rid of your demons? Is the abuse killing you? I want you to quit, son. You need to be around to raise my granddaughter, to walk her down the aisle. Tell me son, will you do that for me?"

"I just don't know how to stop this runaway train," Elvis replied as tears welled up in his eyes. He felt betrayed by his own emotions, surprised the man had been able to coax them out of him so easily. The man had a calming effect on him, and lifted by the thoughts of his mother, he asked, "Can you help me?"

"That's all you needed to say, and that's all I needed to hear," the doctor said with conviction. "Yes, I can help you. I'll be back tomorrow."

"That's it?" Elvis was amazed that the man didn't pry further into the open wounds he had so easily exposed.

"For today it is," the doctor said as he left the room. "And by the way, you need a lot of help."

Chapter 23

The next day, Elvis was once again visited by Dr. Jessup.

"Come in, Doc. Have a seat," Elvis greeted him. "I don't feel so good. I had a rough night last night. So let's just get to it."

"Get to it? Get to it we will," the doctor replied, and both men made themselves comfortable in the seating area. "When did you start taking the pills?"

"Not really sure…" Elvis racked his memory. "Um…late '50s I think, maybe when I was in the army…probably Germany…easy to get anything you want there, especially if you were who I was."

"You started taking what?"

"Well, I've always had problems sleepin'," Elvis said while fidgeting in his chair. "So I took some downers… and then uppers. You could buy amphetamines over the counter back then."

Elvis paused and looked up at the ceiling as if it would help to pull out the memories he'd buried deep in the past. "I remember my mom died earlier that year. It was then, and still is, the most devastating thing that's ever happened in my life, so it was easy to take stuff to make me go to sleep and to get up and stay on the go."

"Okay, so after you got out of the army, what happened?"

"The Colonel had me on the go from the moment I woke up to the moment I went to bed. I was doin' over 150 concerts a year. I was doin' Milton Berle, Ed Sullivan, TV show to TV show, and then cuttin' records. Hell, even my bathroom breaks were scheduled," Elvis chuckled at the absurdity and couldn't help but think of his recent stay in the "detox dungeon." "When I was at Graceland, I slept during the day and stayed up all night. The only time I could go out was when everyone else was in. My life was like a roller coaster that didn't stop until that Mr. Hart snatched my ass and brought me here."

Elvis paused a moment and looked up to the ceiling again. He then looked back to the doctor and said in a very slow, serious tone, "Basically Doc, the world thought I was livin' like a king, but I didn't have much of a life. I felt my life could have changed, should have changed, when my little girl was born in '68, but it didn't. I regret that to this day."

"What about the hard drugs? Pain killers, narcotics? When did they start?"

"I don't remember exactly when it started," Elvis said as he stood up to look out the window, "but I do remember that's when things started getting crazy. I was doin' three movies a year. Everybody wanted a piece of me, and I felt the only time I had to myself was bein' numb."

"By being numbed, you're talking about stoned, right?"

"I suppose. I don't like that word, but yeah, I guess. As I told you before, I've never done illegal drugs. I just took prescriptions from Dr. Nick."

"I get it...Demerol, Dilaudid, barbiturates, they were okay because your doctor said they were? Okay, I got that."

"I know it sounds crazy, but that's just how I saw it. I knew better. I wasn't that naïve."

"Your mother, Gladys, died when you were in your early 20s. I know you were close to her."

"A day hasn't gone by that I don't talk to her, that I don't miss her. I know my life would have been different if she was still here. I would have been happier. I wanted to give her so much."

Elvis sat back down, put his hands over his face, and began to cry.

"You're very depressed for many reasons. That was part of your drug abuse. I know now the inception of your addiction. I can help you reenter this life with a brand-new perspective. What do you say?"

Elvis slowly looked up at Dr. Jessup. "If you could help me relieve this emptiness that I've had for years, then all I can say is yes—yes."

"That's music to my ears," the doctor said while gathering up his things and heading to the door. "I'll see you tomorrow."

Chapter 24

The next day, Dr. Colby escorted Elvis into a large gym filled with exercise equipment. Ten men in top physical condition stood at attention facing him. A tall, muscular man, who was obviously their leader, approached Elvis.

"Working out is one thing," Elvis said as he watched the man with the washboard abs and golden blonde hair approach, "but you don't expect me to look like you, do ya?"

"Good morning, Mr. Presley," the man said in a deep voice that resonated throughout the room. He extended his hand toward Elvis in greeting. "I'm Mike, and those men there are your trainers," he said as he pointed back to the other nine men still standing at attention. "We were hired to get you in shape. First question I want to ask you is what kind of shape do you think you're in?"

Elvis looked at the man in front of him and silently nicknamed him Flash Gordon for another of his comic book heroes. He looked down the line of physically fit men and then looked down at his own stomach, which stuck out much further than it had in his youth. "I'm a little overweight, but I'm okay."

"Really? Well let's go find out," Mike said, and then he led Elvis toward a scale in the corner of the room. When Elvis stood on the scale, the dial settled in on the number 268.

"Well, I guess that's too many peanut butter, bacon, and banana sandwiches late at night," Elvis said. The trainers in the room laughed at the image the sandwich evoked. "Hey, don't laugh at somethin' you haven't tried. It's good stuff."

"Mr. Presley, let me just give you some facts here so we don't have to go over it again," Mike said. "A man with your height, your build, should be 170 to 180."

"Are you shittin' me? You really think I can lose a hundred pounds?"

"I know you can, and we're all here to make sure you do."

Mike took Elvis on a tour of the facility, explaining how the machines worked and what set of muscles each would be targeting. A trainer stood in position beside each of the stations, and

Mike introduced them to Elvis and allowed them to demonstrate their particular machine or set of weights.

"Mr. Presley," Mike said, "I can't do this without you being on a strict regimen with your diet." He led Elvis toward a table at the side of the room where a lovely, young, exotic-looking woman sat. She had light brown skin and golden brown hair which extended in cascades of tightly wound curls well past her shoulders. "Let me introduce you to Alicia," Mike said to Elvis as he motioned for the woman to join them in the center of the room. "She'll be meeting with you to go over your diet, your restrictions, and to make sure you don't have a heart attack on us."

"It's an honor to meet you sir," she said in a pleasant voice. "I'll be meeting with you three times a week to make sure your diet is working out for you."

"Nice to meet you, young lady. Dr. Colby told me all about you," Elvis said with the smile that had won the heart of many a young woman in his day. But just as quick as the smile had appeared, it was quickly replaced with a look of stubborn defiance, and he turned his attention back to Mike. "Y'all really expect me to do this every single day? Work out, eat some shit that I don't want, and just say yes sir, yes ma'am?"

While Elvis was spewing his hatred at Mike and Alicia, Richard silently entered the room.

"So why don't you tell me what you're going to do about it, old man," Richard said. "It's the only way you're getting back to Memphis to see your family. No one even thinks you're alive. Millions are mourning you right now. I have the means to keep you on this island for the rest of your life."

Elvis thought about living his life out on this island, away from the constant demands of the life he had been yanked out of. "Come to think of it," he said, "that's not a bad idea."

"I can make that happen," Richard said.

"You've got to be the biggest dick I've ever known!" Elvis yelled at Richard. He pushed one of the stationary bicycles to the floor. "Do you know who I am? I demand your respect!" He then turned to Alicia and knocked a binder out of her hand, and she jumped back and shrieked. And finally, he yelled into Mike's face, "There was a day I could have kicked your ass as easy as I could spit!"

Mike did not react to Elvis' tirade, but instead stood his ground and stared back, emotionless. Elvis could read people fairly well and knew there was more behind the trainer's blank stare and wanted to push him further, but decided he'd better bide his time for now.

"When I get out of here, each one of you is gonna pay for this," Elvis screamed, and then he pointed at Richard. "But you've got me in a bind." He turned back to Mike and shouted, "So when do we start this shit?"

Chapter 25

Elvis was afforded more freedoms as time went on, and he was eventually permitted to roam the grounds of the compound. He enjoyed walking along the beach, alone with his thoughts. He could always feel the constant gaze of the staff positioned around the site, but he preferred to pretend he was alone. One evening after a grueling workout session, he headed down a wooden path that led through a thicket of bushes and eventually wound its way down to the beach. Before coming out of the shadows of the bushes, he heard a group of the staff members laughing around a campfire. He was curious what was so funny, and he stopped a moment to listen in. He recognized the sound of Alicia's voice.

"He calls me 'ma'am' all the time," she said. "Like 'yes ma'am,' 'no ma'am.' How 'bout 'kiss my ass ma'am.'"

"Yeah, and did you hear him say 'Do you know who I am? I want your respect!'" he heard Mike say.

"I know," another female voice, which he didn't recognize, chimed in. "If I was him with all he has—his fame, his looks, his voice, all that money—there's no way I would have let myself end up like that."

"Yeah, he's basically a junkie," he heard Ronnie, one of the trainers, join in. "Nobody ever says it, but that's what he is—a rich, famous junkie. If he wants off this island so bad, I can get him outta here anytime I want."

"Y'all through yet?" Elvis' voice boomed out from the shadows.

There were several startled screams from the group, and they all stared into the shadows beyond their campfire.

"Oh shit, I think that's Elvis," he heard one of them whisper.

"Mr. Presley," Alicia said timidly. "Is that...is that you?"

"Who else would it be? I was just back there enjoying all those compliments. Well it sounds like my life was pretty much screwed up."

"I'm so sorry...we're so sorry," Alicia said. "We didn't mean that."

"Yes you did," Elvis said as he walked out of the shadows and closer to the campfire. "'Cause it's all true. Don't worry about a thing. I needed to hear all that. I let all that shit control my life, and I'm actually lucky to have what I have. I just didn't realize it. Except for a few people in my life, everyone else around me was sayin' nothin' but 'yes' and lettin' me get away with everything. That's where I miss my mama. She would have never let me get away with one damn thing. If y'all just keep helping me, I promise I won't let any one of you down. I'll kick this thing for good."

"We're sorry, Mr. Presley," Mike said. "I can promise you that we won't let you down either."

"Thanks. I know you won't."

A few of the women were moved to tears, including Alicia, who obviously didn't want him to go just yet. "Hey Mr. Presley, any way you can sing us a song?"

"Oh my God, how embarrassing, Alicia," one of the other women said. "Let him go."

"This is a page right out of one of my movies," Elvis laughed as he walked back toward the group. "Bet ya somebody's got a guitar."

"I do," Mike said.

"Of course you do. I'm waiting for someone to say action," Elvis joked as he grabbed the guitar. "What do you want to hear?"

"I've only heard you sing this song one time," Alicia said. "That was a long time ago—'Forget Me Never.'"

"'Forget Me Never,'" Elvis said. "I haven't sung that in twenty years. That song was dedicated to my mama. Sure. Let me just think of the words for a second..." He paused a moment, then continued. "Okay, I've got it."

While the campfire crackled lightly in front of them and the waves gently crashed upon the shore below, Elvis sang the beautiful song to the group. His smooth voice, the rich tone of the guitar, and the wistful lyrics left the group mesmerized.

"How 'bout y'all just call me Elvis?" he said to the group. "Here ya go, Flash," he said to Mike as he handed him back the guitar.

He then pointed at Alicia. "See ya tomorrow, *ma'am*," he said, and they all laughed in response. As he walked back to his room with a smile on his face, he thought how nice it had felt to have the group laugh with him instead of at him.

Chapter 26

During a brief respite between rain showers, a young boy rode his bike home from school. The sun and the clouds had been fighting for possession of the sky all day. As the last few rays of sun peeked over the clouds before being overtaken again, they lit upon something on the side of the road that glittered and dazzled up at the young boy. He eyed the dark clouds gathering across the field to his right and feared he might not make it home before the next downpour, but the lure of the shiny object proved too much for him to pass by. He hopped off the bike and fetched the object from its resting place amongst the tiny pebbles that lined the side of the road. He turned the object around in his hand and found it was a golden ring with a large diamond in its center, two diamond-encrusted lightning bolts on each side, and the letters "TCB" positioned below. He knew this was no ordinary ring. He tried it on his finger, but it was way too big. Then he tried it on his thumb, but it slipped right off. So he tucked his newfound treasure deep in his pants pocket, jumped back on his bike, and sped off just as the raindrops started to fall. By the time he arrived home, he was drenched. He jumped off his bike and ran through the front yard toward the tiny house where he knew his mother would be waiting in the kitchen. Along the way, his shoes collected a layer of the damp, bright red leaves which had recently fallen from the grove of maple trees across the street.

"Hey Mom," he said as he held up the ring for her to behold. "Look what I found on the side of the road."

"Wipe your feet, Stevie. I told you 'bout that," she scolded him. Then she gasped when she saw what he was holding.

"Son, ya might just want to return this to who it belongs to."

"You know whose it is?"

"I think so," his mother said. "Come on, let's get in the car."

Steve played with the ring as he rode in the car with his mother. He was fascinated with the design and was saddened that he wouldn't be able to keep it. He wanted to kick himself for showing his treasure to his mother, but quickly forgot his disappointment when he realized they were at the gates of Graceland. His mother stopped at the guard gate and rolled down her window.

"Can I help you?" the guard said.

"My son found something that probably belongs to this family."

"Can I see it?" the guard asked. "Oh shit!" he exclaimed when Steve held up the ring. "Why don't you let me have it, and I'll see that they get it."

"I'd rather not. My son found it, and he wants to deliver it."

"Hold on," the guard said. He picked up the phone. "Let me make a call."

"Go on up," he said a minute later, waving them through. "There'll be a few people waiting for you at the porch."

Steve couldn't believe what was happening. He had passed by this mansion many times and often marveled at the fancy entrance. He was fascinated by the design of the musical notes on the gates and the silhouette of a man dancing and playing guitar. As his mother pulled up the long driveway, he could scarcely believe he was now on the other side of those gates.

In front of the mansion, he could see two men and a little girl waiting for them on the steps, but as he and his mother walked toward the small group, he started to lose his nerve and reached for her hand.

"Hi, I'm Vernon Presley," a white-haired man said, and he put his arm around the small girl next to him. "And this is my granddaughter, Lisa Marie." The man then waved his hand toward the tall, distinguished-looking black man on his other side and said, "And this here's Ben. I hear you have something to show us."

"Son, show 'em what you found," Steve's mother said as she squeezed his hand lightly, which helped to steady his nerves.

Steve pulled the ring out of his pocket, stretched out his arm, and opened his hand, revealing the treasure he would soon have to part with. Vernon picked it up, looked at it closely, and nodded his head.

"This was my son's. Where did you find it?"

"Down yonder," Steve said, "on the side of the road, 'bout a mile from here."

"Really?" Lisa Marie said. "Daddy told me he never took it off."

"What was it doin' on the side of the road?" Vernon asked.

"I have no idea," Steve's mom said.

"Mr. Presley," Ben said. "You want me to go down there a piece and check it out?"

"No, no, that's okay," Vernon said. "I'll have Dave check into it."

"Alright then," Ben said with a nod.

"Ma'am, what's your name?" Vernon asked, "And your boy's?"

"I'm Pamela Bourne, and this here's Steven."

"I can't thank you enough for this." Vernon said. "If there's anything I can do for ya, please don't hesitate to ask. Do me a favor, can you leave your name and number with the guard when you leave? I'd like to send you something just to say thank ya."

"Yeah, thanks," Lisa Marie said.

"Oh that's nice of ya, but we're doin' just fine," Pamela said. "We just wanted to return something that I knew meant a lot to this family. Just wanted to…" she smiled up to the group and winked. "Take care of business."

The group laughed at what his mom had said, but Steve couldn't understand what was so funny. He wouldn't learn until later that the letters "TCB" on the ring had stood for "taking care of business," a favorite motto of Elvis'.

As they pulled out of the driveway, the rain began to fall again, and a flash of lightning lit up the sky. Though the ring was no longer in his possession, whenever a storm illuminated the sky, he would remember the glint of the ring he had discovered at the side of the road on that stormy autumn day.

Chapter 27

There was a calendar on the wall of Elvis' room at the island, and he would place an "X" across each day before going to bed. The days stretched into months, and Elvis began to settle into the routine of his life on the remote island. His physical withdrawals had gradually faded away, but his mental addiction to the substances continued to plague his thoughts. He continued his sessions with Dr. Jessup, who skillfully unwound the grip of the impulses which the drugs had woven tightly through the recesses of his brain. He reacquainted himself with the slimmer face that looked back at him in the mirror, but he couldn't quite get used to the natural color of his hair. The stark blue-black color he'd arrived at the island with gradually faded away, and in its place emerged shades of light brown mixed with patches of gray. Elvis also continued to work with the trainers to improve his physical health. He no longer dreaded the times when Mike, or Flash as he now called him, would lead him to the scale. In fact, he quite often found himself standing sideways, looking at himself in the mirror, glad to see his hard work paying off as the bulge of his stomach slowly dwindled away.

He had developed an easy rapport with several of the staff but still had a deep resentment for the young billionaire holding him captive. Elvis would often stare up to the house overlooking the ocean and wonder about the man. Richard held his cards close to his chest, and Elvis couldn't read him as he could most. He knew Richard was likely looking down on him from the large windows above, since he'd heard the man was once again on the island.

Elvis was seated by himself in the cafeteria when he spotted Richard. He stuck his fork into the lean cut of beef in front of him, which he was actually enjoying immensely, and held the fork up toward the young man. "You ever tasted this crap you feed me?"

"No, and I wouldn't want to."

"Well, I see who's the boss around this place," Elvis said, and he then took the opportunity to pry open the guarded exterior of his adversary. "Don't you think it's time for me to know something more about you? Seems like you've known every move I've made in the last twenty years. I don't even know if you're married, got kids, have a girlfriend—so what's the scoop?"

"No, I'm not married. Hell, I don't even have a girlfriend."

"Say what?" Elvis said, and then he shook his head in disbelief. "A good lookin' kid like you? Come on now, tell me the truth."

"I am," Richard said with a laugh. "My parents were on me all the time to get married and quit running around with all those girls, but the reason I couldn't get close to anyone was that I just didn't want a girl who wanted me for my money. You get what I mean?"

"Who do you think you're talkin' to, son? Of course I know what you mean. That's the story of my life," Elvis said. He reluctantly allowed himself to feel for the guy. "The most down-to-earth woman I ever met is Lisa Marie's mother, Priscilla. She didn't care who I was, what I was, or how much money I had. That woman really loved me, and I threw it all away."

Elvis sat back and folded his hands behind his head. He put his feet up on the chair next to him and decided to give the poor guy some advice that could only come from age and experience. "So the only advice I can give you is just let it happen. If you meet a girl, don't tell her who you are. Date her for a while...go to simple places…take her on a picnic or to a church function. Don't spend too much money on her. Hell, did you ever see my movie *Clam Bake*? I played the son of this oil tycoon. I went to Miami and took on another name tryin' to find a girl who would love me just for me and not for my money. That's what you've gotta do."

"Yeah, I saw it, just like I saw every one of your movies three times over. You know, that doesn't sound so bad. That just might work."

"People thought that movie was crap, but maybe it's gonna get you a girl. Let me know what happens."

"You'll be the first to know—other than her—if there ever is a her."

Chapter 28

Back from one of his many trips to the island, Richard was once again in Memphis. He had spent the afternoon with his team, heads down during a working lunch at a local restaurant, planning the expansion of one of his clinics in a remote West African village. Richard was preoccupied with the project. A severe drought and now a plague of locusts had wreaked havoc on the construction timeline. As he headed out of the restaurant, he stopped at the coat check desk to retrieve the heavy wool coat he'd need to withstand the frigid winter air outside. The desk was empty, and after waiting a moment, he decided to head back and find his coat among the many that lined the long rack. While he searched for his jacket, he heard the bell at the counter ring, and he looked back to see the young girl who had recently started at HR standing at the counter.

"Can you get my coat?" she asked, holding her ticket out to him. "Here's my ticket."

"Ma'am, I don't—" he started to correct her and then stopped himself.

"You don't what?" she prompted him.

"I don't believe in love at first sight..." he said, and he immediately wanted to retrieve that line. *Did I really just say that?* he thought. *Guess I might as well jump in with both feet while I'm at it*, he prodded himself to continue. "But I just might make an exception."

He was surprised when the young lady blushed and appeared to respond to his feeble attempt at making a memorable first impression.

"That's an original," she said. "I've never heard that line before. What's your name?"

As Richard prepared his response, he ran through multiple scenarios in his mind, and after what seemed like an eternity, decided to take Elvis' suggestion and conceal his identity.

"Nick," he answered. He'd always liked that name and thought it had a strong masculine ring to it. "And what's yours?"

"Atalynn."

"Well, Atalynn, you don't know me, and I don't know you, but I sure would like to take you out to dinner sometime."

"You would?"

"Sure would."

"Well, I gotta hand it to you," she said. "You sure do work fast. Okay, pick me up after work tomorrow."

"And where is that?" Richard was forced to ask, and he suddenly felt overwhelmed with the enormity of the ruse he had begun. How could he, the CEO, conceal his identity to this girl?

"Just down the road a bit," she answered, "at Hart Health Industries."

"Um..." he stuttered. He pushed himself to continue what he'd started. "What time?"

"How 'bout five?" she said. "I'll be outside. What do you drive?"

"Um—um, it's a white car," he blurted out, knowing he couldn't possibly pull up in the red jaguar he normally drove. "I think it's a Dodge...Can I get your number?"

Atalynn wrote her number down on a matchbook sitting on the counter while Richard retrieved her coat using the number on the coat check slip to find it.

"Here's my work and home numbers," she said as she handed him the matchbook.

"See ya tomorrow," he said, and he slipped the coat over her shoulders.

Richard leaned back against the counter and watched as she walked out. A sudden gust of wind blew her chestnut hair around her face, and he soaked up the last glimpse of her as she walked out of sight.

Chapter 29

Lane walked through the busy newsroom offices of the Memphis Gazette and headed toward the editor's office. He normally loved the buzz on the newsroom floor, with the ringing of phones and the clicking of the keyboards and the whir of the carriage returns on the state-of-the-art electric typewriters, but today he had a knot in the pit of his stomach as he approached the editor's office. He had picked up a message from his boss, Travis, earlier that day and was dreading the meeting to come. As he walked into his boss' office, he saw Travis sitting with arms folded and a scowl on his face, and Lane just knew he would soon be handed his pink slip.

"Grab a seat," Travis said, and he motioned to the chair across from his desk.

As Lane took the seat, it reminded him of the many times during his youth he'd been called into the principal's office. Those visits usually ended with the principal's large wooden paddle whacking him on the rear end, and he could rest assured his daddy would soon top it all off with a whack of his own.

"Look Travis," Lane said. "I know I've screwed up here recently, and I don't blame you if you shitcan me. I know I've been messing up assignments. I wouldn't blame you if you got rid of me. Hell, I'd fire myself."

Lane held his breath and waited for Travis to speak, but Travis just sat there with his arms folded and stared at him.

"Can you at least say something?" Lane broke the silence.

"Lane…" Travis said and then trailed off with a sigh.

Lane could tell the man was having a hard time picking up the axe and letting loose the fatal blow. He watched as Travis fought for the right words and caught a slight glimmer of hope as the man's eyes betrayed the fondness he held for Lane.

"Even though we should get rid of your sorry ass," Travis said, "I'm gonna give you one last shot. And I stuck my neck out for you, so you'd better do this right."

"Really?" Lane said with a shock.

"Yeah, really," Travis said, and then he sighed. "And it's simply because you're a fantastic journalist. But you've been a wreck this last year."

"I know," Lane said, nodding in agreement.

"Your work has been sloppy. You don't turn in your assignments on time. You've been coming into the office all sluggish, and probably drunk, but we decided to give you one more shot," Travis said while shaking his head. "Jesus, I might get my ass chewed out for keeping you, but when your head is right, you're very damn good. This is an easy-ass assignment. All I want you to do is interview the Presley family for the anniversary of his death, which is coming up in a few months."

"An Elvis assignment?" Lane said, thankful for whatever assignment was thrown his way. "Hell, I'll take anything. You know I've never really liked doing these puff pieces, but I need to prove to you and myself that I can be in top form again. This piece will be a winner."

"It better be, because if not, your ass is gone!"

"I got it. When do I start?"

"Right now," Travis said.

"How do I set up this interview?"

"Call Dave Carson," Travis said, and he handed him a slip of paper with a number written on it. "He's Elvis' friend and assistant."

"Thanks boss, you won't be sorry."

Lane hurried out of the office and back to his desk. He grabbed onto the assignment as though it were a lifeline. He picked up the phone and punched in the number.

"Mr. Carson, my name is Lane Bishop," he said. He then rattled off the rest of his spiel without coming up for air, fearing if he gave the other man a chance to interrupt, his cause would be lost. "I'm a reporter for the Memphis Gazette, and we would love to have an interview with Lisa Marie and Vernon Presley for a tribute article we're putting together to mark the anniversary of Elvis' death. I'm calling in hopes that you could help me set up this interview. It will be a very sensitive and tasteful piece, and I would allow Vernon and yourself to do a final review before it's published."

"I don't see why not," the man on the other end said. "Sounds pretty good to me." Of course I have to talk to Vernon and see what he says. I'll need to find out when Lisa Marie is visiting. I think it's pretty soon. How 'bout you leave your contact info with my secretary, and I'll get back with you as soon as I find out."

"Perfect. Thanks," Lane said. "Hope to hear from you soon."

Chapter 30

Lisa Marie sat on the floor with her doll in her lap in the middle of the music room at Graceland. She liked to sit by herself there and pretend her father was still alive. His tender voice sang out "Are You Lonesome Tonight" from the speakers. When she had found the old 45-speed record tucked away in her mother's scrapbook earlier that day, she couldn't wait to place it on the old turntable she knew was still sitting in the corner. As she listened to the song, she reached for the TCB ring which she now wore around her neck. She closed her eyes for a few moments and lost herself in the sound of his voice. When the song was finished, she sat down at the piano, placed her doll next to her, and lightly touched a few keys.

"Hey punkin, can you come on in here," she heard her grandfather call from the next room. "They're here for the interview."

When she walked into the room, she saw her grandfather sitting on the sofa next to Dave Carson, whom she knew well, but sitting in the chair across from them was a man she had never met.

"First of all, let me thank you so much for letting me do this," the man said to her grandfather. "I've never met you or your granddaughter, so I wanted to first say how sorry I am for your loss. The Gazette is doing this as a tribute to your son..." he said, and then turning to her, "and your father." He looked back to her grandfather. "This won't take long at all. I just need to ask a few basic questions, if you don't mind."

"Thank you for those nice words, and you're welcome," her grandfather said. "And I think it's a really good thing that your paper's doing."

"Thanks. My first question is how's everybody holding up?"

"The outpouring of so much support and love for my son throughout the world has given us a good feeling and has helped our family get through this ordeal. I'm doin' okay. I loved my son, and I know he's with his mother right now and that they're looking down and watching over Lisa Marie, and I know he's at peace."

"Thank you for that, Mr. Presley. And what about you, Lisa Marie; how are you doin'?"

"I know my daddy's watchin' me. I hear him sometimes talk to me, makin' sure I do the right thing," Lisa Marie said, and then she held up the ring for him to see. "Plus, I have him right here close to my heart."

"What's that?" the reporter asked.

"That's my daddy's ring. Somebody found it a few months ago on the side of the road and brought it to us."

As the reporter took a closer look, Lisa Marie noticed that Dave Carson looked upset.

Dave was in shock as he looked at the ring. "Oh shit," he mumbled to himself. *I'll be damned, that is his ring. How in the world?*

"I don't know all the details about your dad," Lane said to Lisa Marie, "but isn't that the ring he never took off?"

"Yeah, I guess. But it was found, and maybe he dropped it. All I know is I have it right next to me, and it makes me feel good."

"Oh I forgot, Dave; I wanted to talk to you about that," Vernon said.

I need to shut this thing down, and quick, Dave thought.

"Well, is that about it?" Dave stood up and held his hand out to Lane, who stared back at him in stunned silence.

"Well, I have a few—" Lane started to say but was quickly cut off again.

"No," Dave said. "I think that'll be perfect for your story."

After staring daggers at Dave for a few seconds, Lane looked back to Vernon and Lisa Marie. "Okay, I want to thank you," he said as he closed his notebook in disgust. "I want to thank both of you for takin' the time to answer some of my questions. I know you'll like the article," Lane said, and then he looked directly at Lisa Marie. "Your dad was a great man."

"I know he was," she said.

Dave escorted Lane through the front doors and shook his hand, eager to get rid of him.

"What was that all about?" Lane asked.

"Look buddy, you're lucky you even got to interview them. Just make sure you do this right."

"I'll do the best I can with as little as I got, no thanks to you," Lane said as he headed down the steps.

When Dave walked back into the house, he couldn't hide his irritation when he asked Vernon, "Why didn't you tell me about the ring?"

"And why should I? It was none of your business," Vernon snapped back. "But I do want you to find out why my son's ring was on the side of the road."

"Sure thing," Dave said coolly, reigning in his emotions. "Can I use the phone for a minute in the back office?"

"You know where it's at."

Dave walked to the back office, closed the door, and picked up the phone.

"Hey, how 'bout dinner tonight? Gotta talk to you...it's important. Seven o'clock, same place. Okay, bye."

* * * *

Later, Dave and Richard were huddled together at a corner table in the restaurant which had now become their regular meeting spot. They used this out-of-the-way place to discuss the progress of what they jokingly referred to as *Operation Teddy Bear*.

"We have a serious problem," Dave said to Richard. "That interview I told you about the other day, well it went sour."

"How sour?" Richard asked.

"During the interview, I found out—and so did the reporter—that some kid, about two or three months ago, found Elvis' TCB ring where we abducted him. Lisa Marie's wearing it on a necklace right now. The reporter seemed a bit suspicious."

"And why is this the first we've heard of it?"

"'Cause no one told me about it."

"Could this be a problem?"

"Don't know. I don't know this reporter. Depends how good or bad he is. It's just a tribute article. I doubt this guy's gonna go anywhere with it."

"It doesn't matter," Richard said. "I can't have anything derail what we started. Keep on top of this and fix what needs fixin' if it gets to that point."

"Will do," Dave replied, and he made a mental note to track down the PI he had used in the past.

Chapter 31

The next morning, Lane sat at his desk and doodled on a notepad. He wrote out the letters "TCB" over and over again, trying to put his finger on what it was about the ring that seemed off. He tapped his pen on the notepad and looked up to the ceiling. *Dave Carson, what an ass*, he thought. He replayed the interview in his mind, trying to figure out what he'd done wrong. It always came back to the ring. *Something stinks.* He got up from the desk and approached a woman sitting a few rows away.

"Hey Anna, you still an Elvis nut?"

"Always will be," she said, and she pointed out the memorial she had arranged on her bulletin board. There were pictures of Elvis, newspaper clippings, magazine articles, and lyrics from songs. Lane knew he had come to the right person.

"Let me ask you something. Is it true that Elvis wore some kind of ring that he never took off?"

"Sure is. TCB—that was the ring—takin' care of business."

"Oh. Okay," Lane said.

"Why do you ask?"

"Oh I was just thinkin' 'bout something. Thanks, Anna."

Lane went back to his desk and called Dave Carson.

"This is Lane Bishop from the Memphis Gazette," he said. "May I speak with Mr. Carson? Thanks." While he waited for Dave to come to the phone, he traced over the letters "TCB." When the other man picked up, he said, "Mr. Carson, one more question. That kid who found Elvis' ring on the side of the road, any chance you know where he lives? I want to talk to him for this story. I think it would be a great addition. How can I get ahold of him? ...Oh that's too bad...Thanks for your time anyway. Bye." *Yep, he's definitely an ass*, Lane thought as he picked up his coat, determined he'd get his answers one way or the other.

A short while later, he pulled up to the gates of Graceland and rolled down his window. "Is there any way I can talk to Mr. Presley for a few minutes?" he asked the guard.

"Is he expecting you?"

"No, I just forgot to ask him something in the interview yesterday. You remember me, don't you?"

"Yeah, I remember you, but sorry. No can do."

"Well maybe you can help me. Did some kid come here a few months ago and mention something about Elvis' ring?"

"Oh yeah, I remember him. He and his mom showed up here. When they showed me that ring, I almost pissed my pants."

"Damn, really?" Lane said, and then he immediately tried to get the mental image out of his mind. "Well, anyway, I wanted to interview that kid for my article about Elvis."

"Bet ya he would love that. I know where he lives. They left their address."

The guard wrote the address down and handed it to Lane.

"So cool. Thanks," Lane said.

As Lane drove off, the guard picked up the phone.

In his office a few miles away, Dave Carson answered.

"Mr. Carson, you wanted me to call you if that reporter ever showed up again," the guard said.

"What did he want?"

"Oh, it was no big deal. He just wanted to find out where that kid lived that brought the ring a few months ago."

"And what did you do?" Dave said. The tone of Dave's question was more accusatory than curious, and the guard knew he was in trouble.

"Gave him the address?" the guard timidly replied.

"You did what?" Dave exploded. "Tell me you're jokin'!"

"Was that a problem, sir?"

"Now it is," Dave said, and he slammed down the phone. "Damned reporter," he said to himself. "Dolly, come in here!" he yelled to his secretary.

"Oh no, what's wrong?" she said.

"Do we still have the number for that PI?" Dave asked when she entered the room, and he shot her a look to let her know not to pry any further.

"I think we do."

"Call him. Tell him to get his ass in here as soon as possible."

Chapter 32

It was late at night on February 1st, and the sounds of the island's nocturnal creatures could be heard above the crashing waves on the shore. Elvis had grown accustomed to the nightly serenades from the cicadas and frogs. Though they kept him awake at night, he didn't even mind the familiar sound of the mockingbirds. It was the occasional screeching of the large seabirds that drove him crazy. He stood in front of the calendar on the wall and prepared to mark off another day. As he started to make the "X," though, he paused, sat down on the bed, and put his head in his hands. "Today's her tenth birthday," he said aloud to himself. He thought of the last time he'd seen his daughter: when he had brushed the hair from her face while she lay sleeping like an angel. He then sighed, turned off the light, and let the sounds of the island lull him to sleep.

* * * *

The next morning, Elvis was on a bench pumping weights, and Ronnie was spotting for him.

"Did you mean it?" Elvis asked.

"Mean what, sir?"

"That you could get me off this place anytime you felt like it."

"What are you talkin' about?"

"I overheard you say that a few months ago at the beach, around the campfire. The night I surprised y'all, remember? Did you mean it?"

"Maybe."

"Can you come by tonight?" Elvis asked.

"Maybe."

* * * *

That night, Ronnie came to Elvis' room as requested.

"I need you to cut through all the bullshit," Elvis said, "and be straight with me. Can you do it?"

"Depends what you can do for me."

"I knew this was comin'. How much?"

"Two fifty?"

"If you get me off this island, and soon, it's all yours, not a problem."

"I don't know; this is so risky. I know you'll want to bring down Richard after you get outta here. The feds'll be swarming this place, and I don't want to be caught up in that."

"How 'bout 300?" Elvis offered. He hadn't met a man yet that money couldn't buy.

"You twisted my arm."

"So what's the plan?"

"In that case," Ronnie started, "let me tell you what I've mapped out. We have to do this at midnight, two nights from now. That gives me time to get ahold of a friend. Midnight is important, 'cause that's when the staff changes shifts. I'll be here at 11:55, right outside your window. Four of your window bars will be cut to the point that it will look like normal, but all you have to do is push them, and they will bend. We'll go through those woods," he pointed to the dark jungle on the other side of the meadow, "then down to the beach, where I hid a boat. There'll be a compass in the boat, and all you'll have to do is point it north. You take off, and in ten miles, approximately one hour, you'll reach a small island, where there's a lighthouse. You can't miss it. From there, you'll be picked up by a friend of mine who will take you to Miami. Once you're in Miami, you're on your own."

"It's that simple? No guards roaming the grounds? No dogs? Nothing?"

"Guards, dogs—what do you think this is, a maximum security prison?"

"It is to me."

"The medical staff hands off their shift report at midnight," Ronnie said, and he continued to lay out the details of his plan. "We have a five-minute window to run 200 yards straight from here to that wooded area. I'll help you halfway through, and then I gotta get back. It's not that far from where I'll leave you to get to the shore and the boat. Once you're in Miami, the first call you make will be in front of my friend to transfer the money to the account number he gives you."

"That's a pretty elaborate plan for someone who needed his arm twisted so hard. I think I had you at two fifty."

"That was my plan too."

"Good plan," Elvis said. "No more talk. I got it. I'll see you outside my window at 11:55 two nights from now. Get outta here before you're missed." Elvis held out his hand to Ronnie, and they shook to seal the deal.

"Okay, it's on," Elvis said. "See ya then. Don't back out on me."

"Not for that kinda money," Ronnie said.

Chapter 33

Two nights later, Elvis was once again alone in his room, pacing the floor. He watched the clock as it got closer and closer to the appointed time. He walked up to the calendar on the wall and pointed to Feb 1st. "I'll see you soon, darlin'," he said.

When the clock reached 11:55, he turned off his lamp so the room was lit only by moonlight. He opened the window and looked out into the dark. He could see the silhouette of Ronnie waving to him from a few yards out.

"You ready?" Ronnie whispered.

Elvis nodded, grabbed the bars on the window, and began to push. They slowly bent forward until there was enough room for him to crawl through. As he jumped onto the ground, Ronnie urged him on. "Hurry up, let's go."

"Hell, I'm tryin'," Elvis said as he picked himself up. They ran across the compound grounds and into the wide meadow beyond. Elvis had studied the stretch of land carefully earlier in the day. He knew he would run just north of the helicopter and slip into the dark jungle at a point between two large palm trees. Elvis was surprised at his stamina. His legs carried him along at a good clip, and he had no problem keeping up with Ronnie. As they reached the dark recesses of the jungle, Ronnie turned on a flashlight.

"Stay behind me," Ronnie said as they ran deeper into the thick jungle.

After a few hundred yards, Ronnie stopped. He shined his flashlight on one of the trees and showed Elvis a red mark painted across the tree's trunk. "You see that?" Ronnie said. "I've marked the way with red paint on the trees every twenty yards. I've gotta get back."

"What?" Elvis said. "That's your plan on getting me out of this hellhole?"

"It's your only way," Ronnie said, and he held out the flashlight for Elvis. "Follow the marks. You'll be out of here in ten or fifteen minutes. The boat's waiting for you. Good luck."

"Damn, I hope this works out better than last time," Elvis said.

As he stood alone in the jungle, the sounds of its nocturnal inhabitants grew in intensity.

He heard skittering noises at his feet, the rustling of branches above, and the sounds of wild creatures of the night from every direction. He closed his eyes for a moment to settle his nerves, then pointed the flashlight in the direction of the beach and started on his journey. His progress was slow, being hindered by the thick growth of the jungle that slapped at him as though protesting his invasion. He felt he was being stalked by some invisible predator, hidden by the darkness of the jungle, and this prompted him to quicken his pace. Unfortunately for him, he didn't see the slick mud in his path before it caused him to slip. When he crashed to the ground, he lost his grip on the flashlight, which broke open upon impact. The light he had depended upon had now been extinguished.

He fumbled around in the dark for several minutes, and though he eventually found the flashlight, he could not find all of its batteries. He decided he'd better keep moving toward the beach. As he started to walk toward the sound of the crashing waves, he rubbed his knee, which had been banged up pretty good during the fall. Without the flashlight to help guide him to the red markings of the trees, he had only the dim moonlight and the sound of the waves to guide him. He walked slowly with his arms in front of him to avoid running into anything, a precaution he wished he'd thought of before bumping his forehead on a tree branch. Eventually, he spied an opening through the trees, and beyond that he saw the moonlight shining on the water.

As he emerged from the jungle, he spotted a small boat a few hundred yards down the beach and limped in its direction. When he reached it, he stared at it for a second and then kicked the sand in front of it. "This piece of shit's gonna get me there?"

In the distance, he heard the first piercing blares of the sirens coming from the compound. He quickly grabbed the front of the boat and pulled it into the water. He waded out several yards into the ocean and jumped inside, lowered the small engine into the water, and pulled the cord. It sputtered. He kept pulling the cord to no avail, and after the fourth pull, he yelled. "For $300,000, you better start, you piece of ..."

He pulled again with all his might. It started.

Chapter 34

Atalynn had gotten over the nerves she felt during the first few days on the job and had grown close to her supervisor, Sally, and her coworker, Lyndell. They often ate lunch together in the gardens outside their office. Today was one such day.

"Tell us all about him," Sally said to her. "Don't leave anything out."

One thing Atalynn had learned about Sally was that she had a way of prying things out of her. She didn't mind, though; she liked how it felt to open up to the woman. Today, Sally was curious about the date Atalynn was going on after work. Atalynn knew the woman wouldn't be satisfied until she had described Nick and their chance encounter in exhausting detail.

"Okay, okay," Atalynn said. She could feel both women lean in closer, not wanting to miss a thing.

At that moment, Richard walked into the arboretum from the opposite side of the building. He had planned to rush through the gardens to get to a meeting he was running late for, but as he started over the large stone bridge in the center of the gardens, he spotted Atalynn and her friends sitting on a bench that faced the bridge on the other side. He quickly backpedalled and concealed himself behind a fringe of wisteria that clung to an arbor at the front of the bridge.

From the fourth floor window, Julie looked down at the gardens below and found Richard's behavior odd and decided to amuse herself at the sight of his obvious discomfort.

"His name is Nick. He works at the coat check desk at a restaurant," Richard heard Atalynn say. "He fed me the corniest line ever: 'I don't believe in love at first sight, but I think I'll make an exception.'"

As the women laughed, Richard felt his cheeks flush with embarrassment. *I think she nailed that impression*, he thought, and then he braced himself for the next onslaught.

"But I couldn't resist. He was so adorable. He has light brown hair, or maybe it's blonde, and green eyes. He's tall, with broad shoulders. And I remember his voice. There was something about his voice that made me melt."

He heard the other women say "Awww" in unison.

"He's picking me up outside after work. We're going to dinner."

"Sally, you and I are gonna be out there watching," he heard Lyndell say. "We can't miss this."

"No we can't," Sally said. "Sounds like Robert Redford's picking her up."

The three women laughed and began to pick up their belongings to go back inside.

"Hey, Atalynn, I need to introduce you to someone over in Finance," he heard Sally say. "Let's cut through the gardens, it's on the other side."

Upon hearing this, Richard ran to the far side of the bridge and attempted to hide himself behind several large boulders, but he lost his footing and slid into the water below, creating a loud splash.

"What was that?" Atalynn asked.

"Don't know. Maybe one of those goldfish got a little frisky," Lyndell said.

Richard stood in the water below the bridge and waited for the women to pass. As soon as they exited the courtyard, he pulled himself up the side of the bank and made his way back to his office.

Julie had found the whole scene to be quite amusing and had laughed so hard she'd spilled her coffee. She quickly headed back to her desk outside of Richard's office and waited for him.

"What was that all about?" she asked as he appeared in the doorway.

"What?" he asked.

"That comedy skit I just witnessed in the gardens. I haven't laughed so hard in months."

"Very funny," Richard said, and he sat down with the dejected look that always brought out the motherly side of her. She had known him since he was a kid and had a soft spot in her heart for the man.

"So which of those girls were you hiding from?" she asked. "I'm guessing it was that new girl in HR. The one you had me send the flowers to. Why were you hiding?"

"You're going to think this is the stupidest thing you've ever heard, but I met her the other night at a restaurant, and she didn't know who I was. I just got carried away, and the next thing I knew, I had pretended to be the coat check attendant and introduced myself as Nick."

"Oh Richard," Julie said as she shook her head. "What have you gotten yourself into?"

"I know. And that's not all. I made a date with her. I'm supposed to pick her up in front of the building today after work. And I'm supposed to be in an old white Dodge."

Julie couldn't help herself, and she began to laugh. "I'm sorry, honey, but this is hysterical. I'll tell you what, I'm gonna help you. My brother's got a beat-up old Dodge. I'll have him drop it off in the parking lot. It's yours for the night."

* * * *

After work, Atalynn walked out of the office building and looked for Nick. She spotted an old white car parked quite some distance down the street and assumed it must be him. As she approached the car, she could see Nick sitting in the driver's seat with sunglasses on, wearing a baseball cap pulled way down over his forehead. He exited the car and walked around to the passenger side and held the door for her.

"Your chariot awaits," he said, and he flashed a wide grin.

"Why thank you, kind sir," she said with a giggle.

From their vantage point in front of Hart Health, Lyndell and Sally watched the exchange.

"Hey, is that Mr. Hart?" Lyndell asked.

"Are you kidding?" Sally said. "Richard Hart driving a car like that? Can't be."

"Yeah, I guess you're right."

Julie had also made her way down to the front of the building. "Ladies, that can't be Richard," she said. "I just left him upstairs."

Chapter 35

In the warm waters of the Caribbean, in the dead of the night, Elvis was moving along at a good clip. He had one hand on the rudder, and the other was holding a compass. The salty brine of the sea sprayed up on him as the tiny boat cut across each wave that rolled toward the shore he had left far behind. The tune he quietly hummed was from one of Lisa Marie's favorite cartoons, and he looked forward to watching her laugh at that silly show while he held her in his lap. The thoughts of Lisa Marie and his home in Memphis were cut short, though, when the engine started to sputter.

"No. No! Don't you dare do this to me!" he yelled.

The engine stopped, and the silence enveloped him. The only sound was the light lapping of the waves that lifted the boat gently up and down. Elvis reached for the cord attached to the engine and pulled. Nothing. He pulled again. Nothing. He stood up to get better leverage and pulled up on the cord with all his might, and it broke away from the engine and knocked him off balance. He tried to catch himself from falling backwards but tripped on the small bench across the center of the boat. He put one hand down to try to break his fall, and the other hand, which held the cord, flew up over his head. He held onto the cord's handle for dear life, knowing he would need to reattach it to the engine to have any hope of starting this damned boat back up again.

As he lay in the bottom of the boat trying to gather his senses, he felt a tug on the rope that he was still holding tightly in his grip. He tried to pull it back toward him, but there was a resistance preventing him from dislodging it from whatever was holding it. He righted himself and sat up on the little bench and yanked the cord, which gave up a little slack, but then he heard a hissing noise coming from the front of the boat, and an enormous iguana stood up on its hind legs and lunged at him with its mouth opened wide.

"What the hell!" he yelled, and he jumped to the back of the boat. He fumbled around and found an oar lying at the bottom of the boat. The lizard was bobbing its head up and down wildly and thrashing its long, spiked tail from side to side. Elvis swung the oar at the monster and sent it flying into the water. He watched as the creature swam away and saw the cord, wrapped around its tail, gliding behind.

He sat back down and pounded the boat with his fist. "Why can't anything go right?" It was then that he spotted a small box beneath the bench. He pulled it out and found it had a big "E" written on top. Inside, he found a bottle of pain-killers with a note that read: 'Thought you might want this. —R."

"What a jerk," Elvis said as he crumpled the note and threw it into the ocean.

Elvis pondered his next move, knowing there wasn't a next move. He opened the bottle and poured several pills into his hand and stared at them. He looked around, and in all directions he saw nothing but the vast expanse of the ocean. "If I'm goin' down, I might as well go down in flames...I tried darlin'...I almost made it."

As he raised a handful of pills to his mouth, he suddenly heard a voice.

"Hey boy, you sure you want to do that?"

"Oh shit!" Elvis yelled, sending the pills flying in all directions.

"I'll let that pass, seein' how I just popped up here."

"Hey, it's you," Elvis said to the figure sitting across from him, who wore a Memphis Tigers T-shirt and a baseball cap. "You're the guy from my dream."

"No dream, son. You're out in the middle of the Atlantic, nowhere to go, in a decrepit little boat," the angel said as he looked around at the boat, shaking his head in disgust. "You were gonna pay a quarter million for this?"

"Actually it was three," Elvis said, and he held up three fingers.

"Looks like you're up a creek without a paddle, so to speak."

"Yeah, looks like it. I guess it was a stupid plan, but I'd do anything—I'd give anything—to be with my little girl again."

"I believe that," the angel said. He pointed upward. "And so does he. I'll see ya soon."

"What?" Elvis was surprised that the figure had vanished as quickly as he'd appeared. "Where'd you go? God, please save me, please save me."

A bright flash of lightning forked across the sky, and a deafening roar of thunder shattered the silence. A strong wind came up, and Elvis had to lean into it to keep his balance as the boat rocked violently. Raindrops pelted his face, and he had to grab the edge of the boat to avoid being tossed into the ocean.

"God, please save me. I need to see my little girl before I die. I'll do anything you ask of me. I promise I'll change...please save me."

Elvis felt the tiny boat being lifted by an enormous wave, and he lost his balance. A vision of Lisa Marie flashed in his mind right before he hit his head on the side of the boat. Blackness replaced the laughing face of his daughter, and he lost consciousness.

Chapter 36

With Julie's help, Richard had settled on a little burger joint outside of town as the spot for his first date with Atalynn. He felt bad taking her to such a dive but wanted to let this thing play out as planned. They sat at a cozy booth, getting to know each other over burgers and fries. She had a way of joking with him that disarmed him, and as the evening wore on, he felt his guard gradually drop away.

"So tell me about yourself," she asked as she propped her elbow on the table and rested her chin in her hand, giving him her full attention.

"Not much to say," he began. "I'm from an average family. I'm an only child. My parents were killed in an accident a few years ago." *Okay, well most of that was true*, he thought.

"Oh, I'm sorry," she said, and he could sense her sincerity.

"I am too, but I'm doing the best I can. I'm working odd jobs trying to save up some money. Not exactly sure what I want to do, but I'm figuring it out as I go along. Maybe an office job somewhere is in my future. What about you?"

"I was born and raised right here in Memphis. I have an older sister. I'm sure my parents were hoping I'd be a boy—at least my dad did—that's probably why he dragged me around to half the fishing holes in Tennessee. I didn't mind, though. I went to school in the area and got a business degree and just started a new job at Hart Health Industries."

"They build hospitals, don't they?"

"They do. One guy owns it, Richard Hart. I've never met him. From what I hear, he's a pretty nice guy. One day he's gonna hear about me, though. I plan on working my way up all the way to the top level one day."

"I believe one day you will."

"Urgent call for Richard Hart," a page came over the restaurant speakers. "Please come to the front desk."

"Hey, that's who I work for," Atalynn said and started looking around. 'He must be here. I've never seen him."

Richard squirmed in his seat, pretending to look for whoever was getting up to answer the page. "Can you excuse me a sec?" he said. "I need to go to the restroom."

"Sure."

Richard got up and walked to the front desk, which was hidden from Atalynn's view by a wall. He told the hostess that he was Richard Hart, and she handed him the phone.

"What?" he asked the person on the other end of the call. "Okay...I'll be there before dawn."

"Is something wrong?" Atalynn asked when Richard returned to the table.

"I was just thinking about a friend that I'm having some problems with," Richard said, and he wondered how she'd read his mood so easily. "I've been trying to help him through a rough patch in his life, but he's fighting me at every turn. I don't know what to do. I'm thinking it might just be time to bow out and let him figure it out for himself. I don't know what to do."

"Is he a good friend?"

"Not a close friend, but he was important to my family, especially my dad."

"Well, I'd help him then. If he's goin' through a rough time, I'd help him. You never know, one day he might come back around and help you."

"You know, he already did," Richard said. "So now it's my turn. You're right. Thanks. That helps."

* * * *

Later, when they walked to the car in the parking lot, Richard unlocked her door and held it open for her. As he headed over to the driver's side, he heard the lock on his door release and smiled that she had thought to reach over and undo it for him. On her part, she knew it would signal the young man that she was enjoying his company. Her mother had taught her the importance of the many little signals she could drop to a man to let him know she was interested without being overly flirtatious.

When he walked her up to the door at the end of their date, he leaned over and kissed her on the cheek.

"I hope you had good time," he said. "I know I did. Can I call you again?"

"You better," she smiled up at him. "I hope everything turns out okay for your friend."

"Me too."

After she closed the door, Richard could still smell the scent of her perfume, and he carried thoughts of her with him throughout the long flight to the island.

Chapter 37

Light waves lapped at Elvis' hand, which hung off the side of the boat. He began to stir and raised his hand to his face to block the sun. He started to sit up but then grabbed his head, moaned, and laid back down face-first in the boat. After a few minutes, he pulled himself up on his hands and knees and looked out upon the vast waters in front of him, but as he turned slowly around, he saw the white sand and the jungle trees behind him. His boat was lodged on the same shore that he had taken off from the night before. He didn't think he'd ever be glad to see the place again but found himself shouting for joy as he jumped out of the boat and into the shallow water.

As he splashed toward the shore, he saw a brightly colored iguana with a cord wrapped around its tail saunter slowly into the jungle. Elvis laughed at the sight. He walked onto the beach, limping and disheveled, and looked up to the clear blue sky. "You kept me alive, and I'll keep my promise."

* * * *

"I see him! There he is! It's Elvis," one of the staff yelled, pointing toward the jungle. In the distance, Elvis emerged from the trees. He walked with a limp toward the compound and looked very ragged, scratched up, bloodied, and bruised. Two of the staff members ran up to him and attempted to assist him, but he motioned them aside.

"It's okay. I can do it myself."

He walked across the wide open meadow toward the compound. He looked to his left and saw Ronnie being escorted by two men into the compound. He looked up to his right and saw Richard standing on his balcony, smoking a cigar, staring down at him.

From his balcony, Richard had watched as Elvis emerged from the jungle. He had picked up the phone. "Hey Doc, check him out, make sure he's okay, and then send him up here." He had then lit a cigar and watched as Elvis trudged back to the compound.

* * * *

Later, Richard and Elvis sat together on two cabana chairs on that same balcony and looked out at the beautiful turquoise waters that stretched out for miles.

"You want a Cuban?" Richard said as he held out a cigar.

"Love to, but don't tell Flash." Elvis joked.

"It's all good, he works for me."

"Now that's a good cigar," Elvis said as he leaned back and pulled in the first puff, enjoying the rich, spicy aroma.

"How you feelin?" Richard said. "Looks like you got banged up."

"I'm alright," Elvis said, and then he looked Richard directly in the eye. "Look, I don't need any more bullshit from you. I want to get this done right. I know I'm not ready to go home yet, but I do know it'll be soon. And I plan on working my ass off from now until you say I'm ready, but let me warn you, it had better be soon."

Both men felt the shift in their relationship at that moment. The load was a little lighter on Richard's shoulders, and Elvis was glad to carry the extra weight that came with being in control of his own destiny.

"Let me ask you something," Elvis said. "Do you believe in God?"

"I always have," Richard said, and he got a faraway look in his eyes. "There've been times in my life I've felt God's hand at play. Other times, I felt alone. But yes, I believe in God."

"Yeah, me too."

They sat in silence for a few minutes, and Richard found himself thinking of Atalynn again. "You said you wanted me to tell you," Richard said. "I had a date last night in Memphis...I really liked her. She told me I should help you, and that's what I've been trying to do and what I'll keep on doing."

"She sounds like a keeper to me," Elvis teased the young man.

"And by the way," Richard said, "if you ever meet her, my name is Nick."

They both laughed.

"All joking aside, though," Richard said. "I've been helping you for more than just yourself. It's for all of us who see you as the King of Rock. That's why I want to bring you back. It would mean so much."

"I get it. This is bigger than just about me. I get it," Elvis said, and he winced as he pulled himself up from the chair. "I need some rest, and I'll hit it hard in the morning."

"One more thing," Richard said.

"What now?" Elvis said and plopped himself back down in the chair.

Richard reached into his pocket and threw something at Elvis. A silver coin tumbled head over tails as it flew across the room. Elvis reached up and caught it mid-flight. When he opened his hand, he saw a nickel with the worn outline of a buffalo.

"Remember that?" Richard said while Elvis stared at the coin.

"Hart...Richard Hart..." Elvis said. He slowly looked up to Richard and pointed at him. "You're that kid."

"Yeah. I'm that kid."

"I don't know what to say," Elvis said. "I feel like this last year has all been a dream. I don't know what to say to you Richard, to thank you for saving my life."

"There's nothin' to say. I don't know what would have happened to me if it wasn't for you, if you hadn't been there to save me."

"I remember your parents," Elvis said, and he puffed his cigar. "They were both so worried they'd lost you that night. What was your father's name?"

"Andrew."

"Oh my God, Andrew Hart," Elvis said as another connection to the man dawned on him. "You know, your father named a wing in the hospital after me?"

"Well of course I do. He felt a great debt to you, Elvis."

"It was him, wasn't it?" Elvis asked. "It was him that set all this up."

"It was. I just took it over."

"You took it over?"

"Yeah, they were killed in a car accident three years ago. I miss them every second, every minute, every hour of every day."

"Oh man, I'm sorry," Elvis said. "I'll bet you do. I'm really sorry about that. I know how it feels to lose a parent." Elvis leaned back in his chair. "I've got a story you should hear, and you might not believe it, but I'm gonna tell you anyway. One morning last year in my room, they tell me I had a heart attack. I could see Dave tryin' to save me, and I went somewhere outside of my body. I met what I think is an angel, and he showed me the day that I saved you back in that parking lot so many years ago. He told me I was gonna have a second chance in life, and he said it was because of you. To tell you the truth, I barely heard you cry that night because I was so distracted doing other things. It was the angel that intervened back then and led me to rescue you. So when you mentioned the hand of God in your life, that was one of those times. The angel reappeared to me last night on the boat, and I knew then that it wasn't a dream, it was real."

"I believe you," Richard said. "It seems God has given us both a second chance at life."

"It seems that way. And I made some promises that I'm gonna keep," Elvis said. "You know, my mama always said that if I was good to somebody, that somebody might come back and do good to me. Mama was always right. It was you she was talkin' about." At that moment, both men felt their mothers' presence on that remote island in the middle of the Caribbean.

* * * *

When Elvis got back to his room, he found Ronnie on his hands and knees, surrounded by cleaning supplies, scrubbing the bathroom floor. "At least I got a clean toilet, and it only cost me my pride," Elvis teased Ronnie, who scowled back at him.

Joyce peered into the room. "When you're finished with those floors, I heard the kitchen needs some help with the dishes. Speed it up boy, you've got a long list of chores to finish before you make up for all the trouble you caused."

Chapter 38

Lane had followed the guard's directions and now found himself on the front steps of a modest little house not far from the Graceland estate. A bicycle lay in the front yard as though it had been hastily discarded. On one side of the yard, a rake lay near a large mound of brightly colored leaves that looked as though they had been dive-bombed or used as a wrestling mat. And on the railing around the porch, there was row after row of tiny little green army men strategically placed in mock battle. *I think I've found my man*, Lane thought as he looked about and waited for someone to answer the bell. After a few moments, a woman answered the door, and Lane explained what he was there for. The woman called to her son, and they walked with Lane out to the street. The boy told Lane how he had found the ring, and he pointed Lane toward the spot where he had discovered it. Lane thanked them both, shook their hands, and jumped back in his car.

Lane found the spot, just as the boy described it. He got out of the car and kicked the dirt on the side of the road and looked through the grass. Something caught his eye, and he bent down to retrieve it.

Nearby, someone else watched through binoculars as Lane bent down and picked up a syringe, placed it in his pocket, and climbed back in his car.

* * * *

That same someone watched as Lane approached the house of Joel Cooper later that night.

"Good evening ma'am, my name is Lane Bishop. I work for the Memphis Gazette," Lane said to the woman who answered the door. "I'd like to start out by saying how sorry I am for the loss of your husband. I'm working on a story for the anniversary of the death of Elvis Presley. I would like to ask you a few questions, if you wouldn't mind. You are his widow, aren't you?"

"Yes, that's me. The name's Brooke, but this needs be quick," she said as she looked past him down the street. "I...I'm pretty busy."

"Your husband also perished in this tragedy, and I would like to include some information about him in this article as well."

"Like what?"

"I would like to know what kind of relationship your husband had with Elvis. How often did he fly for him?"

"I...I don't know. I have no idea."

"Did he ever talk about him? How often did he fly him? Once a month? Once a year? Anything I can use?"

"Um, I think Elvis' regular pilot got sick, and they called Coop that day. He just didn't talk much about what he did. All I knew...all I knew was he was a private pilot, and he flew people around."

"You mean he didn't tell you he was flying Elvis Presley? At midnight? On the night of the tragedy?"

"Maybe...I'm not really sure. That's—that's all I know."

"Is that Daddy?" a little boy said as he ran up to Brooke. He looked expectantly out the door, but his face dropped when he saw Lane.

His dad? Lane thought. *That's weird*.

He looked back at Brooke, who had put her arm around the boy.

"No, he's not comin'," Brooke said to the boy, and she pointed him in the direction he had come. "Go back to your room, Gavin." She then looked at Lane and whispered, "He's still having problems with the loss of his father."

"I understand," Lane said. He could have sworn he heard the little boy say, "But he promised," as the boy left his mother's side.

"Well, I appreciate your time," Lane said. "I'll let you get back to what you were doing. I see you have your hands full."

As Lane walked away, he thought what a complete waste of time it had been to come out here. He lit a cigarette and got back into his car. He leaned back and stared at Joel Cooper's house. "Something is just not right," he said to himself. "It just doesn't add up. I think I'll just sit right here for a bit."

A few minutes later, he saw headlights approach from a distance, and as the car neared, it pulled into the driveway of the Cooper residence. He watched as Joel Cooper exited the car, and he watched as Brooke opened the door, looked around nervously, and motioned the man inside.

A few minutes later when Coop emerged from the house, Lane was waiting in ambush. He popped out from behind a bush. "Thought you blew up with Elvis," he said, startling the man.

"You must be that nosy reporter," Coop said after regaining his composure.

"Mr. Cooper, why don't you tell me what really happened?"

"Look man, I can't, and I won't talk about it."

"Okay. Fine. This will be in the paper tomorrow. That I found you—alive."

"No, no, no. I just—I just can't talk about it. Why don't you ask Dave Carson?"

"Dave Carson? What's he have to do with it?"

"Just talk to Dave. I've gotta go."

Through a set of binoculars, someone had watched as the scene unfolded.

* * * *

A few minutes later, at a nearby gas station, Coop entered a phone booth.

"Dave, you're gonna kill me," he spoke into an answering machine. "I know you told me not to go home, but I had to see my kid. It was his birthday. I just wanted to see him for a few minutes. There was some reporter that ambushed me. His name was something Bishop. I didn't know what to say. I said I couldn't talk about it and that he should talk to you. Man, I'm sorry."

Chapter 39

"I found Joel Cooper alive and well last night, as you already know," Lane yelled at a startled Dave Carson. "So what the hell's goin' on?"

"What are you talkin' about?" Dave yelled back. "And how dare you just barge into my office like this?"

"I'll tell you what I'm talkin' about. You either faked his death or murdered Elvis."

"What are you accusing me of?"

"I don't have my facts yet, but I know you had something to do with faking Mr. Presley's death, or you had something to do with his murder."

Dave stood up, pulled out a gun from the drawer, and pointed it at Lane. "Which butt cheek do you want this bullet to go in, right or left, while you turn around and get the hell outta here?"

Lane walked backwards to the door with his hands held up. "Whoa, take it easy."

"Mr. Bishop, watch your back," Dave said as he put the gun down on his desk. "Now, get out!"

* * * *

"I know it's early," Richard said as he escorted Dave into the drawing room at the Hart Estate, "but do I need a drink before you tell me what's going on?"

"Yeah, you better make it a strong one."

"Okay," Richard said, and he poured himself some Jack Daniels. "Lay it on me."

"I've had a PI following that reporter since he learned about the ring. First of all, he talked to the kid who found the ring. Then he went to the sight of the kidnapping, looked around, and found the syringe we used to sedate E. I guess it dropped during the struggle, just like the ring. Then he went to Coop's house to talk with his wife. And are you ready for this? Idiot Coop shows up, and the reporter confronts him. Then Coop says, 'Talk to Dave Carson.' The reporter barges into my office this morning and accuses me of faking Elvis' death or having him killed."

"We have to contain this before it gets out of control," Richard said while he topped off his drink. "One more thing, Dave; don't ever let me hear you call Coop an idiot again. That man's a hero, and my friend."

"Yeah, I know. Sorry 'bout that. It won't happen again. And what did you mean by 'contain this'?"

"Call your boys," Richard said. "That reporter needs a short vacation on a beautiful island."

"I was afraid you were going to say that. Okay. Damn, this is gettin' way too deep."

"Set it up and make sure he's on the plane tonight no sooner than 2 a.m. I need to be there a few hours before him to explain everything to Elvis."

Dave got up to leave and looked back at Richard. "Don't drink the whole bottle."

* * * *

Later that night, Lane frantically ran down the hallway of his small apartment. He was being chased by four unknown men. He had been sleeping on his sofa, a usual occurrence since Teresa had left him months earlier, when a loud pounding at his door awakened him. As he had gotten up, planning to spy out the peephole, he had watched the door being kicked in, and four men had rushed inside. That's when he took off in the only direction available to him, away from the door and down the hall.

As he reached the end of the hall, in a split second, he chose the door on his left, the bathroom. He quickly locked the door and ducked down, propping himself against it in an attempt to strengthen it.

"Open the damn door!" he heard one of the men shout from the other side.

"Before we bust that shit in!"

"What do you guys want?" Lane screamed, and he eyed the small window on the wall above the toilet.

"Open the door now!"

"Hell no!" Lane yelled. He then found himself flying across the small room and crashing into the bathtub as the men kicked in the door.

"Get the hell off me!" he yelled as they grabbed him and pulled him out of the bathroom.

"Shut your damn mouth!" one of the men barked.

"What do you want from me?" Lane yelled as he struggled to escape their grip.

"If you stop fighting us and come, you'll be fine!"

Lane continued to struggle, but stopped abruptly when one of the men slugged him in the stomach. "Suit yourself," the man said.

They dragged him out of the apartment and toward a van in the parking lot below.

"This is kidnapping!" Lane shouted as the unknown men threw him in the back of the van. His hands were then tied, tape was placed around his mouth, and he was blindfolded.

Chapter 40

"Did I win the lottery?" Lane jeered as the blindfold was removed from his eyes. The bright sunlight blinded him for a moment, and he had to grab the rail of the stairs which he was so rudely being pushed down. When he was about halfway down the set of stairs, he was finally able to catch his balance. He shielded his face from the sun with his hand and gazed with open-mouthed amazement at the island paradise in front of him. "Where the hell am I?"

"Shut up," one of the two goons escorting him said. "Get in the Jeep."

"I thought I'd be met by a limousine," Lane taunted, not about to let these assholes know how scared he was. "Somebody is gonna regret this big time."

"Buddy, you've got no idea. Now get in the Jeep before we throw you in."

"God, I need a drink," Lane said.

Lane was driven from the airstrip on a road that led into the thick jungle and wound its way down a long hillside. He could see an opening in the trees below and saw a sunny meadow stretching out to the ocean, but the Jeep turned up a driveway to the left. A few minutes later, he was escorted into the living room of a large house nestled on the hillside.

"Sit in this chair," one of the two men commanded.

"What the hell is going on?" Lane asked. He was irritated and shaken. "Where's my drink?"

"No alcohol on this island."

"I knew I was in hell."

From his chair, Lane could see the ocean out of the large sliding glass doors that led onto a balcony. *What is this place?* From his left, he caught a movement and turned to see a man enter the room.

"What the fu—" he started to say, but then he realized who the man in front of him was. "Are you Richard Hart? The Richard Hart?"

"In the flesh."

"Why am I here? What just happened? And why are you here?"

"Calm down, Mr. Bishop," Richard said, and he raised a hand toward Lane to let him know he was expected to stay seated. "Let me explain what's going on, and let's see if we can work things out. You got too close to a story that I needed stopped."

"What? So let me get this straight. I get my door kicked in, dragged out of my apartment and dumped into a van, gagged and tied, thrown into a plane, and I'm on some god-forsaken island all because of a story?" Lane said as he gave a white-knuckled death grip to the arms of his chair. "What the hell kind of story could possibly justify what just happened to me?"

"The Elvis story."

"The Elvis story? I knew I was right. So I'm brought here to keep my mouth shut?"

"Well, sort of. I'll explain it to you in just a sec. I have an exclusive interview that's going to take your career to another level," Richard said, then he motioned to one of his employees. "What you're about to see is what dreams are made of. It's something that you only see in movies. Bring him in."

What dreams are made of? What I only see in movies? Lane thought. *This whole thing feels like a movie, or a nightmare.* A second man emerged from the hallway and sauntered into the room and stood directly in front of him. The light filtering in through the large window behind the man created a silhouette effect, but as the man's face came into focus, Lane jumped out of his chair.

"Holy shit! Elvis? I—we—thought he was..."

"Dead?" Elvis said. "Not hardly."

"Did I die?" Lane wondered aloud.

Richard and Elvis couldn't contain their laughter, and they both fell onto the sofa in stitches.

"How bad do you need a drink?" Richard asked Lane.

"Really bad."

"Then you're not dead, Mr. Bishop. Can I call you Lane?"

"Call me whatever you want."

"Look, I needed to save Elvis' life. I don't want to get into the details, but I can't let anyone find out that he's still alive, and if you wrote your piece, a lot of people would have had suspicions. I can't risk that."

"Why did you fake his death? What was the point? What about the plane explosion?"

"I was kidnapped, same as you," Elvis said, and he frowned at Richard. "I was already on my way to the island on a different plane when the Lisa Marie exploded. Thanks a lot for that, Rich."

"Have you watched any TV in the last six months?" Richard asked Lane. "Or heard any radio?"

"Oh Lordy, Lordy, mercy sakes," Lane said, running one hand through his hair while he pointed the other at Elvis. "This is the May 24th? That's what all those ads are about? Now doesn't that just take the cake?"

Lane watched as Richard and Elvis laughed again and sensed the two men had become close friends since the night of Elvis' kidnapping. They acted as though they were old buddies, having a good laugh at his expense.

"What Elvis has agreed to do in exchange for your silence is give you an interview any time you want on this island and after The Event, but you've got to keep things quiet. Don't write anything about him until after your last interview. You can stay here a week and have full access to the compound."

"Damn, this was my last hope of keeping my job," Lane said, dejected. "I've got to write something soon, or my boss will fire me."

"How much do you make a year?"

"Twenty-eight thousand."

"Tell you what, before you leave this island, I'll triple that," Richard said. "You go tell your boss you quit. That way, when this story comes out, you can sell it to anybody in the world for millions."

"You've got yourself a rock solid deal," Lane said as he got up and extended his hand to Richard.

"Well, Mr. Bishop," Elvis said. "You ready to become the most famous man in the news world? Let's go for a walk on the beach. Ask me anything you want. Let's go take care of business."

Just yesterday I was in my apartment in Memphis, and now I'm going for a walk on the beach with Elvis Presley. Doesn't that beat all? Lane thought as he and Elvis walked down toward the beach.

* * * *

"Mr. Presley," Lane said as they walked along the beach.

"Call me Elvis."

"Tell me what you've been doing for the past six months."

"Have I got a story for you. It started the night I was leaving for my US tour."

Lane reached into his pocket and took out his notepad and pencil and prepared to capture the details of the greatest story of the century.

Chapter 41

Lane pulled up a chair to the side of the Olympic-sized pool where Elvis was swimming laps. Mike stood at the pool's edge with a stopwatch in his hand. As Elvis touched his hand on the side of the pool, Mike clicked the stopwatch.

"So how'd I do, Flash?" Elvis asked.

"Great! Three seconds better than yesterday."

"Yes!" Elvis said, and he lifted his hand in the air in triumph. He then pulled himself out of the pool, grabbed a towel, and dried off. He walked over to Lane and struck a pose like a body builder. "How do you like the new me?"

"You mean the old you?" Lane said.

"That's what I meant."

"Well, I'm leaving this afternoon," Lane said, and he thought how unreal this still seemed. *Watching Elvis swim laps*, he thought. *Crazy*. "I got almost everything I need, but I just want to go over a few things with you. I've been playin' around with a few different titles for the article I'm gonna write about you. So let me give 'em to ya, and let me know what you think. Here's the first one: *Elvis, the Return of the Crown*," Lane said.

"Uh," Elvis said, giving him a thumbs-down. "What's the next one?"

"How 'bout *The Billionaire and the King*?"

"Keep goin'," Elvis said.

"Well, this is my last one: *Saving the King*."

"You know, I never really talked about this to anybody, but I never took to that title. I'm just a country boy who could carry a tune and was given a chance by Sam Phillips at Sun Records. I know that Johnny, Carl, Jerry Lee, Roy, and all the rest, we all owe our success to that man. I was just at the right place at the right time with the right song. And I'll tell ya one more thing. If Mama heard people call me the King of Rock 'n' Roll, she would have nipped that in the bud. She would not have liked it, but I love my fans, and if that's what they want to call me, then that's what I am. So let's go with *Saving the King*."

"Can I quote everything you just said?" Lane asked.

"We gave you full access. Do what you wanna do."

"When I was interviewing Richard a few days ago," Lane said, "he told me somethin' that maybe he should tell ya, but I've just gotta do it."

"What is it?"

"There's one more person that gave Richard the final push to continue with his father's plan to bring you here."

"Who was it?"

"He's a good friend of yours, and he's been through the same hell as you."

"Oh my God, the man in black. It was Johnny, wasn't it?"

"Sure was."

"Johnny and I were always good friends, but now I realize how good a friend he was."

"I can't thank you enough for what you've done for my career," Lane said, "and I just want to tell ya, I didn't start out this way, but I'm one of your biggest fans."

"Well thank you very much," Elvis said, doing an exaggerated impression of himself.

Lane laughed a moment, but then he took on a more serious expression. "Seeing what you've overcome has given me hope that I can dig myself out of the hole I've turned my life into. Alcohol has ruined me and messed up so many things I cared about in my life."

"I'm glad you mentioned that. I've been wanting to talk to you about it. Look, you've been here a week without any alcohol, and I know it's been rough. Richard is going to call you tomorrow when you get to Memphis, and he's taking care of everything to get you help. Promise me that you'll follow through with it, and I promise you that you can call me any time and come over any time, and we both can help each other."

"So I can come over to Graceland and talk to you any time I want?"

"That's what I said."

"Like I said to Richard last week," Lane said, "you've got yourself a rock solid deal." Lane stood up to leave. "All I need now is to talk to Dave, and I can wrap this thing up." He extended his hand to Elvis.

"Yeah, I need to talk to him too...in a bad way," Elvis said as he shook Lane's hand.

I just want to tell my old school buddy "Thank you for havin' the courage to kick my ass into gear," Elvis thought, *but I'm gonna make him sweat a bit before he drags it outta me.*

Chapter 42

"What is it, Dolly?" Dave Carson said into the intercom on his desk.

"Lane Bishop is here to see you."

"I was expecting him. It's okay. Let him in."

"Have a seat, Mr. Bishop," Dave said when Lane walked in. "So how was your vacation?"

"Oh that vacation that started with two of your goons throwing me in a van?" Lane hissed.

"Yeah, that one. I told you to watch your back."

"You sure did, and you also had a gun pointed at my ass."

"That gun had no bullets," Dave said with a chuckle. "So what can I do for ya? Richard told me to answer all your questions."

"That's why I'm here," Lane said.

"Ask away."

"Look, you Neanderthal, I'm not here to forgive and forget. You had me roughed up and kidnapped, but I need some background on Elvis' early years, and I know you're the guy with the answers."

"Whoa, hold on. You were not to be harmed. That was not part of the plan. I had it out with my guy over that. And I'm sorry 'bout that, but don't forget who I was workin' for. I was takin' orders from Richard, and you made peace with him. So back off, buddy," Dave said, and he held his hand out to Lane. "Truce?"

"I wasn't really pissed, I was just givin' ya hell. Truce it is," Lane said, and he shook Dave's hand. "I just gotta say, you guys had some balls to do what you did. What you guys did, to get him clean so he wasn't just another tragic story, was selfless. I'm not that religious...don't know if there's a God up there...but if there is, you guys are on the list."

"The guy has the biggest heart of anyone I've ever known," Dave said, "and I knew once he got clean and started thinkin' straight, he'd be on board. I took a big chance that he'd hate my guts. Hell, I haven't even seen him since that night."

"Really? When do you plan on seein' him?"

"When Richard calls me and tells me it's time. And I'm scared shitless. How does he look?"

Lane stood up and walked around the room looking at photos of Dave and Elvis together and pointed to one. "Right there, that's how he looks."

"Oh wow, that was in '69," Dave said. "To me, that was Elvis at his best."

"I want to piece his life together all the way from his early childhood to after his return. Can you tell me about his teenage years?"

"Everyone around him knew there was something special about him," Dave said, and he pointed at a picture of Elvis and himself at a church picnic. "When he sang in the church choir, we were all mesmerized, wondering where in the hell he'd gotten a voice like that. Gospel was his favorite music. He once told me that was the music that spoke to his soul." Dave pointed at a picture of Elvis with his arm around his mother. "And about his mom...do you see that picture right there? That was a year before she died. He's never been the same since."

Dave paused for a moment and searched through his desk and pulled out a picture of Elvis' mom standing in her kitchen. "You see this? Elvis bought her that electric mixer there in that picture. Gladys loved it so much, he bought her another one for the other side of the kitchen. And his father? He wouldn't let anybody cuss around his dad. Hell, you couldn't even say *hell*."

"What about the drugs?" Lane asked.

"I really don't think you should get too much into that," Dave said. "Let him just deal with that without the whole world knowin' every detail."

"I agree with that," Lane said, nodding in agreement. "I'll write something generic about the abuse. I think I have all I need. Elvis told me the rest. Man oh man, I've got the story of the century."

"Yeah, you are one lucky son of a bitch, that's for sure."

"Crazy how life comes around. Thanks for everything, Dave. And I don't ever want to see your goons again. See you at The Event," Lane said, and he got up to leave.

"Get outta here."

Chapter 43

Dave's heart beat rapidly, and he couldn't stop his thoughts from racing as he stood in the hallway outside of Elvis' room. He wanted to think about anything other than what was about to happen, but that was an impossible task. He tried to pull up his mental checklist of the things that needed to be done around Graceland and back at the office, but his mind would not be distracted from this spot outside of Elvis' room. He could hear Richard with Elvis and waited for his cue.

"You look fit, Elvis," he heard Richard say.

"Amazing what can happen when you're forced into it," Elvis replied. "I mean, when you put your mind to it."

Dave heard both men laughing, and then he heard Richard's voice and those dreaded words. "I've got someone that wants to talk to you."

"And who would that be?" Elvis asked.

Dave stood frozen on the other side of the door and found he was unable to move. That was his cue, but he couldn't get his feet to budge. *I can't do this*, he thought, *I'm outta here.* As he started to inch toward the exit door a few yards away, he felt Richard tugging on his arm.

"Get in here," Richard said, and he dragged him back to the open door.

As he stood in the doorway, he watched as Elvis jumped up, clenched his fists, and took several quick strides in his direction.

Richard positioned himself between Dave and Elvis and put one hand out toward each of the men, which had the intended effect of stopping Elvis in his tracks.

"Was wondering when I was gonna see you again, old buddy," Elvis jeered. "Ready to get your ass kicked?"

Dave had been worried how Elvis would react, but he had never feared Elvis in his life until that moment. The man he saw in front of him was seething with anger, and Dave knew if it hadn't been for Richard, Elvis would have torn him apart. Dave was speechless.

"Naw, just kiddin'," Elvis said with a sly smile.

"Whew!" Dave said as he let out a sigh of relief. "I was sweatin' that one. I think you deserve an Oscar for that performance." It was then that he was able to fully appreciate the transformation of the man standing in front of him. "You look great, E."

"Well I better. As of today, I've lost eighty-two pounds."

"Eighty-two pounds...man, I can't get over how fit you look. I'm shocked."

"I'll tell you what really shocked me, is you, brother, doin' what you did. Keepin' tabs on me for decades, workin' for this guy's dad? Wow."

"You know why I did it, don't ya?"

"Yeah, I got it. But there was a point where I wanted to kick more than your ass."

Elvis grabbed Dave, and the two men hugged while holding back tears.

"Hey buddy, let me show you some of my karate chops," Elvis said while he chopped at an invisible target. "I can really kick my legs now."

Elvis went through a series of karate chops and kicks and finally finished with a reverse roundhouse kick that came up just inches shy of Dave's face. "Shazam!"

The three men laughed, and Dave thought how nice it was to see his old friend looking so good and enjoying himself.

"Dave, here's a list of songs; can you get the old band together for that big shindig Richard here's got planned for me?"

"It's already done, but they think they're playing at a charity event with an Elvis impersonator," Dave said, and he thought what a kick it was going to be to see the boys' reactions.

"I hate to break up this little love fest, but I'm heading back to Memphis now," Richard said. "Dave, I'll give you a week, and then I need you back. And you, Mr. Presley, next time I see you, I'm picking you up, and we're going back home."

Elvis and Dave spent the next week working out together, enjoying the sights of the island, and reminiscing about childhood memories that came flooding back now that they were together again.

Chapter 44

Richard felt guilty that he had continued to keep his identity a secret from Atalynn. After their first date, he hadn't had much time to nurture their growing relationship, but his thoughts often drifted back to her. With Julie's assistance, he had avoided bumping into her at work, and he'd had to invent a few interesting cover stories as to why he was out of town so often, but his secret had remained intact; he was still Nick the coat check attendant who worked odd jobs to make a living. His latest cover story was that he had been on an Alaskan fishing trip, earning good money catching salmon. He thought the story was rather inventive, but he was now regretting it. Upon his return from "fishing," Atalynn thought it would be fun if the two of them did some fishing of their own. And that's how he found himself on the banks of a local fishing hole, doing his best to show her how skilled he was at the sport and kicking himself for agreeing to it, since his knowledge of fishing was limited to what he'd seen Marlin Perkins do on the *Wild Kingdom*.

She had provided the bamboo poles, and they had gone together to the bait and tackle shop to pick out the bait. Luckily, she picked up a container of earthworms, and he didn't have to decide what kind of bait would work for catfish, which is what she informed him they'd be trying to catch. He managed to get the worm on the hook and cast the line out like a pro, or so he thought.

Atalynn watched as he cast his line and quietly laughed at how he had barely pierced the worm on the hook. It had most likely fallen right off as soon as it hit the water. She had thought it strange when Nick didn't know what kind of bait would be best for catfish. He had picked up some colorful flies as though they were going fly fishing. That's when she had picked up the earthworms. "Let's use these," she had offered. And now it was starting to dawn on her that he didn't exactly know what he was doing.

"Can you go get my sweater from the car?" she asked, and she offered to hold his pole. While he was on the errand, she secretly retrieved the hook and re-baited it to make sure they'd both have a good shot at catching something.

"Here you go," Richard said as he slipped her sweater around her shoulders. He kept his hands on her shoulders a moment longer than he should have, but he couldn't resist. He was drawn to this girl who looked so natural in her jeans and T-shirt with her hair held up in a ponytail. When he pulled himself away, he took the fishing pole back from her, and they sat side by side, enjoying the warmth of the sun, waiting for something to bite.

Hers was the first line to jump, and she squealed with excitement. She jumped up and pulled it up out of the water and onto the bank. "It's a whopper," she said as she deftly pulled out the hook and placed the fish onto the stringer hanging over the bank.

"Hey, your line's got one too," she shouted. "Pull it in."

I can do this, Richard thought. After all, he had just seen Atalynn do it. *No problem*. He pulled the fish onto shore just as she had done and was disappointed to find his catch was considerably smaller than hers. He looked at that fish and thought how ugly it was, with those long whiskers and that gaping mouth. He thought the whiskers might sting him, so he was careful to grab the fish squarely across its back, unaware that catfish had razor sharp spines. It felt as though a hundred needles had entered his palm, and his reflexes took over and he flung the fish back into the water. *Oh that was swift*, he thought. "It was too small, I decided to throw it back," he said, trying to recover his dignity.

Atalynn watched his antics and became convinced he knew absolutely nothing about fishing. *But hadn't he just spent a month on a fishing boat?* she thought. She grabbed a piece of ice from their cooler, reached for his hand, and held the ice cube over his palm. The sensation of his warm hand and the cold ice cube caused her pulse to quicken, and she had a sudden urge to reach up and kiss him, but she felt him pull back, and the moment passed.

When she had held his hand, Richard too had felt a desire to hold her close and kiss her, but his nerves failed him. He walked toward the bank and picked up a stone, and with a flick of his wrist sent it skipping across the water.

"Wow, you've got some skills, Nick," Atalynn said. "I counted eight skips on that one. Think you could teach me how to do that?"

"Sure. Come on over," Richard said, and he picked out another smooth stone that was perfect for skipping.

She took the rock and sidled up in front of him, and he placed his arm over hers. He guided her hand back and explained how she needed to flick her wrist real fast and try to get the stone to catch the water on its flat side so it would bounce along the top of the water.

"Here, you do it first and let me just see what it feels like," she said as she handed him back the rock and wrapped her arm around his. He wound up and then sent it flying across the water. She laughed, and when she turned around to face him, his arm wrapped around her waist. He bent down...and kissed her tenderly.

It's about time, she thought as his arm wrapped around her waist and his lips touched hers. She would think of that first kiss for many years to come, and she never divulged her own secret: that she could skip a rock with the best of 'em.

Chapter 45

Elvis walked down the hall of the compound and stopped in front of the tiny room where he had spent his first few weeks. He cracked the door open to take a last look inside. He remembered how abandoned and alone he had felt back then, but then he flashed back on the staff that had helped him through those dark hours and realized he had never been alone. People had held him up every step of the way. He closed the door and continued down the hall and out the exit toward the beach. The sun was near the horizon now, bathing the sky in pastel shades of orange and pink as it bid farewell to another day.

"Mama, if you're lookin' down on me, and I know you are, I'm doin' this all for you and my darling little girl," Elvis said as he watched the setting sun. He walked along the shore and felt the warm water of the Caribbean as it ebbed and flowed along his path. He reached down and picked up a small pink and white seashell with scalloped edges and tucked it into his pocket. It was to be a gift for Lisa Marie.

"Since you've been gone, Mama, this is the first time I've felt alive. Hope I'm makin' ya proud. I did what you told me to do. I helped someone in need...a little boy many years ago, and now he's saving my life. I have a strange feeling that you've been guiding that boy all along."

* * * *

Later that night, all the staff on the island gathered in the cafeteria. The room had been re-arranged such that a small section of bleachers was now on one side of the room, the long tables had been removed, and a small wooden stage had been erected along the wall opposite the bleachers. All of the staff members were seated in the bleachers, silently waiting in anticipation. The large double doors next to the stage opened, and in walked Elvis with his trademark jet black hair. The staff had become accustomed to seeing him in sweat pants and loose-fitting T-shirts, but tonight he was wearing snug-fitting jeans and a T-shirt that fell close to his body and hinted at the chiseled set of abs beneath. He hopped onto the stage and approached a large microphone.

"Y'all know I'm leaving tonight," he said. "I want to say sorry for the times I yelled and snapped at ya, and I'm sorry for the times I lied to ya. And for all the dirty things I said. I'm in debt to all of you for the rest of my life—for saving my life. You know where I live, and my doors are open. I've got two surprises for ya. I'm flying all of you to Memphis to watch yours truly at The Event, and the other surprise is being passed out now."

Elvis watched as the staff excitedly pulled out several hundred-dollar bills from envelopes that were being handed to each of them. He saw Richard standing on one side of the cafeteria, quietly watching the excitement.

"Oh hold on," Elvis said. "I got one more thing for y'all. I'm gonna sing you a song, and the boss is gonna help me with it. It's a little something we came up with together. It's called 'The Memphis Island Blues'. Come on up here, Richard," he said, and he motioned to the man standing in the shadows. "Come on."

As Richard made his way slowly up to the stage, he had his hands in his pockets and shook his head. Several of the staff could be seen holding back their laughter.

"You ready, partner?"

"No, I'm not," Richard said as he took a spot next to Elvis on the stage, "but I promised you, so let's do it before I throw up." The staff could contain themselves no longer and burst into laughter.

"Okay, okay, hurry up. I'm gettin' sick."

In a cappella, Elvis sang the first line, "*My name is Elvis Presley...*" He then pointed to Richard, who missed his cue. Elvis stopped abruptly, and Richard smacked himself in the forehead with the palm of his hand.

"Good God, get to steppin', boy," Elvis chided. "Let's try it again."

"*My name is Elvis Presley...*"

Elvis pointed to Richard, who hit his cue perfectly, "*And I am Richard Hart...*"

The staff hooted and hollered in response.

Elvis sang the next line, "*He snatched my ass and tied me up...*"

Followed by another one from Richard, "*And that was just the start...*"

They sang the chorus together: "*It's the Memphis Island Blues, baby. The Island Blues. Come on down with us and pay your dues...*"

They performed the rest of the number together, much to the amusement of the staff.

"I'd like to hear from a few of ya," Elvis said after they finished, "to hear if you still hate me, or if we're cool. Hey Flash," he pointed to Mike, the trainer. "How 'bout you get us started?"

"I just want to say that when we first met," Flash said as he stood up, "and you got right in my face and said you could kick my ass, I was ready for you to bring it on, but then I realized who you were and that you were very ill at that time," Mike paused, looking for the right words. "You've inspired me to work hard and never give up. So thanks. And by the way, you can call me Flash any time you want."

"And what about you, Alicia?" Elvis said to Alicia, who stood up in response.

"Just like Mike said, you've taught me—and I think all of us—that no matter how low you get in life, with help from friends, nothing can keep you down. And when I come to your house, I've got a great low-calorie recipe for a peanut butter, bacon, and banana sandwich I'm gonna make for you."

"Can't wait for that, *ma'am*," Elvis said, and he bowed in her direction. The staff laughed in response.

Elvis spotted Ronnie standing alone against the wall and motioned to him. "Hey Ronnie, come sit down here with your friends. I understand why you did what you did, but I ain't gonna hold it against you. None of us is perfect in this life, and Lord knows I wouldn't be here if

I was. So buddy, it's all good between us. I expect to see you up in the balcony with your friends at my return."

"I don't know what to say," Ronnie said as he took his seat. "Except I'm sorry."

"It's all forgiven," Elvis said, and then he looked for Joyce. "What about you, Joyce? You were the first nurse that took my tongue lashing. How many times have I apologized to ya?"

"With this one tonight, it's sixteen. And I accept. That's enough. But I want to tell you one last thing. What you just did, forgiving that scoundrel, that made this old woman proud."

"Well Joyce, then I just want to thank you again. You've seen me at my worst, and I'm glad that from now on you'll see me at my best. And now y'all, I've got to get outta here soon. I'm really happy I've got some new friends," Elvis said. "And I know that I can call each and every one of you my friends. I don't know what else to say to you, but you're all part of my family now. And I thank you from the bottom of my heart. And one more thing—I know there's a bunch of ya, but can I give each one of you a hug?"

The staff gave Elvis a standing ovation, and then they each took turns hugging him goodbye.

* * * *

As the plane slowly ascended away from the island and into the night sky, Elvis looked down at the bright lights of the compound that illuminated the trunks of the surrounding palm trees. As he looked out at the silhouette of the tall palm fronds to the moonlight playing on the sparkling waters beyond, he silently thanked the Lord that he was finally on his way back home.

He sat in reflection for many long minutes, replaying the last year in his mind and anticipating the new life he was now entering. Eventually, he turned his attention to Richard, who was seated nearby with glasses on, jotting something down in a notebook.

"Whatcha doin' there?" Elvis asked.

"Just working on some of the last details."

"I need to say somethin' to you."

Richard took off his glasses and gave Elvis his full attention.

"I want to say how sorry I am for being such an ass in the beginning, and I want to thank you for what you've done to change my life," Elvis said. "I owe you so much."

"No you don't," Richard replied. "I did this because I wanted to. Seriously, you owe me nothing. I'll tell you who you do owe; you owe your father and Lisa Marie everything. You owe them a different Elvis."

"I'll spend the rest of my life tryin' to make things up to them," Elvis said, shaking his head.

"Oh, and one more thing," Richard said. "I owe you something."

"Like what?" Elvis asked.

"Like a new plane."

"Don't worry 'bout that," Elvis said. "Let's just call it even."

"No. I'm getting you another plane. How about this one?" Richard said, and then with a sheepish grin added, "I need an upgrade anyway."

"Well you know what they say don't you?" Elvis asked.

"No, what do they say?"

"It's good to be king."

"Damn right."

Elvis laughed, leaned back, and closed his eyes.

Richard stared at Elvis for a few moments and he, too, reflected on the past year and all that had been accomplished.

Chapter 46

Richard walked down the large staircase that led from the main house down to the pool area behind the large mansion of the Hart Estate. He saw Elvis lying on a lounge chair, soaking up the sun beside the large pool that looked like it had been erected for the Roman gods. He watched Elvis looking around at the lavish grounds surrounding the pool. There were marble statues adorning either end of the pool, and the entry to the nearby pool house was fashioned after an ancient temple.

"This is an awfully big spread for a bachelor. I think I see some children in your future," Elvis teased.

"You never know," Richard said. "You ready for tomorrow?"

"Never been more ready. So the world thinks I'm dead, huh?"

"Dead as a doornail," Richard replied, and he peered at Elvis over the top of his sunglasses. "Why?"

"You know, this is probably my one last shot to feel like a normal person before I step into that limelight again," Elvis said as he stood up. "I need to borrow your car."

"Borrow my car?" Richard said, and he jumped out of his chair, prepared to go toe to toe with Elvis. He'd be damned if Elvis was leaving. Not when they'd come this far. When he looked at the glint in Elvis' eyes, though, he relented. He didn't want to stand in the way of him walking through the world anonymously for one day. "Which one?"

"One that won't stick out."

"Take the '65 Mustang," Richard said. "We're so close to finishing; are you sure you want to do this?"

"I just wanna feel normal. And while I'm at it, I've been eating that health nut food for a year now, and I want something I can sink my teeth into."

"The keys are in the glove box. It's parked in the fourth garage."

* * * *

Elvis rolled down the window and turned on the radio as he wound his way down the driveway of the Hart Estate. He breathed in the scents of the spring grasses and marveled at the beauty of the countryside. He turned the radio up for one of his favorite Bob Dylan tunes and heard the announcer mention that tomorrow would be Dylan's 37th birthday. *Well happy birthday, Bob*, he thought. *Now there's a true talent.*

Before long, he pulled up to a Burger King on the outskirts of the city. As he walked in, he could feel the stares of a few people in the small dining area and did his best to ignore them as they whispered to one another and pointed in his direction.

"I'll take a Whopper, fries, and a large Pepsi," he said to the girl behind the counter.

"Excuse me," a woman tapped him on the shoulder. "I know you've heard this before, but you look just like—"

"I know, like Wayne Newton," he interrupted, trying to deflect her suspicions.

"No," she laughed. "Elvis Presley."

"Really?" he said, pretending to be shocked.

Elvis grabbed his food when his number was called and headed back to the car. He immersed himself in the typical American fast food meal and savored every bite. He wanted to cruise through downtown Memphis before he headed back to Richard's, but a sign on the side of the road caught his attention: Elvis Impersonator Contest, noon today.

This should be fun, Elvis thought. He pulled into the parking lot and watched as several Elvis wannabes milled around, waiting for the doors to open. There were young Elvises, old Elvises, skinny Elvises, and fat Elvises. Some were dressed in his early '50s look, with a black dress coat and sporting his famous hairstyle, with the top of their hair swept high over their foreheads while the sides of their hair were slicked back away from their faces. Others were in the more flamboyant costumes of his later years, with rhinestones and fringe adoring their outfits and heavy sideburns lining their jaws. There was even a little boy Elvis and a few female Elvises. He couldn't help but laugh at the sight. *Now these are what I call devoted fans*, he thought.

When the doors opened to the event, he decided to wander in and amuse himself with the spectacle of it all, but as he entered the building, he was handed a number, and before he knew it, he was standing in a line with all of the Elvis hopefuls. His jeans and T-shirt didn't exactly fit in with the spirit of the contest, but he couldn't resist seeing how this would play out. He heard a group of contestants nearby comparing notes on their costumes and scoping out the competition. He saw a group of them looking him up and down and snickering. They walked up to him and gave him a scathing critique.

"Elvis never dressed like that," one of the men said. "What are you dressed as, James Dean? This is an Elvis contest. You look more like Wayne Newton than Elvis Presley."

"Elvis never wore his hair like that either," another one chimed in.

Elvis put his hand through his hair and scratched his head with a perplexed looked on his face. "Have any of you guys ever been to one of my—I mean one of Elvis' concerts?"

"We all have, dummy, and we're telling you, you don't look like him. Boy, looks like you're gonna have to gain about thirty or forty pounds and have one of those nose jobs—rhynocasty, plasty, whatever they're called—if you want to look like him."

"You really think so?" Elvis asked and touched his nose. *Maybe if I shake my leg they'll recognize me*, he thought. "Hey guys, look at this," he said, and then he swiveled his hip and shook his leg. The group laughed in response.

"Are you havin' a seizure, boy?" one asked.

"Tough crowd," Elvis said under his breath.

"Can all the Elvises line up against the wall?" an announcement was heard. The contestants then lined up, and three judges with clipboards approached. They began interviewing Elvises one at a time, starting with the leftmost contestant. From his place in the center of the line, Elvis watched as a few select impersonators were asked to go to the other side of the room, while a greater number of contestants were dismissed. When the judges reached Elvis, he had to fight back his laughter.

"What's your name?" the first judge asked.

"People call me Elvis," he replied.

"Sure they do, but what do you call yourself?" the judge prompted.

"Elvis," he said, and he had a hard time keeping a straight face.

"Looks like we've got a live one here," one of the judges whispered to another.

"Have you ever performed in front of an audience?" the second judge asked.

"Thousands of times, I suppose," Elvis replied.

"I'll bet you did," the judge said while rolling her eyes. "Now give us your best impression of Elvis saying 'Thank you very much.'"

Elvis cleared his throat, pointed his finger at the judges, and in his deep, distinctive voice said, "Thank you very much."

"Thanks for coming, but maybe next year. Go home and get some more practice."

"Well then, I'm leaving the building," Elvis said, and he headed to the door while the judges shook their heads.

This has got to be one of the weirdest moments of my life, he thought.

Chapter 47

Richard pulled up in front of Atalynn's house in the same beat-up old white car he'd borrowed from Julie. He watched Atalynn get up from the porch swing and walk down the front steps. She was wearing a sundress with a tight-fitting bodice that cinched at the waist, accentuating her feminine curves. The rose colored pattern brought out the blush of her cheeks, and the red highlights in her hair sparkled in the late afternoon sun. As she walked toward the car, Richard was mesmerized.

"Don't get out of the car, it's okay," Atalynn said as she opened the door and slid inside.

"You sure look pretty tonight," he said.

"Well thank you," she said. "And you look rather dapper yourself." She leaned over toward Richard, who met her halfway for a kiss.

"No matter what happens tonight," he said as he reached for her hand, "promise me nothing will change between us."

She took his hand and looked up at him, admiring the handsome good looks of the man beside her. "Why would you say that?" she asked.

"Oh, I don't know," he said as he gently squeezed her hand. "Just talking crazy. Let's go."

* * * *

When they approached the large auditorium in the heart of Memphis, a huge throng of people was crowded in front of the building and spilling out onto the surrounding streets. It took quite a bit of maneuvering, but Richard eventually inched the car to the security gate at the back parking lot. When he had invited Atalynn along, he had told her he would be a stagehand working the event. He rolled down his window, and one of two guards in the booth bent down.

"Passes please," the guard said while his partner behind him peered over his shoulder.

"Hey man," his partner said. "That's Mr. Hart. Let him through."

"What did he say?" Atalynn asked as the guards waved them through.

"I'm not sure..." Richard tried to recover. "Something like, 'Bless his heart, let him go through.'"

"That's silly," Atalynn giggled.

When they reached the backstage door, one of Richard's employees was waiting. Richard held Atalynn's hand and ushered her along in front of him while he secretly placed his finger to his lips, signaling his employee to stay quiet. "This guy's going to take you in and show you where to sit down in the back," Richard said to Atalynn as he ran his hand down the side of her cheek. "Like I said before, I've got to go inside and take care of some stuff. Is that okay?"

"Of course it is, Nick. See you soon," Atalynn said, and she kissed him.

The employee motioned for Atalynn to enter the building in front of him and looked back at Richard with a quizzical look on his face. Richard whispered, "Don't say a word."

Richard watched as the door closed behind them, and he stood on the back lot for a few moments trying to settle his nerves for what was to come. At that very moment, there were people all over the world turning on their televisions in anticipation of The Event. They had been bombarded with a daily reminder about the mysterious event for a year, and the suspense could be felt in every living room across the country and throughout the world. Production crews at every major news station were cuing cameras and preparing sound equipment. In front of the auditorium, news crews were jockeying for position. Pre-show speculations abounded.

"Ladies and gentlemen," a young female reporter spoke into a camera, "tonight's the night the whole world has been waiting for, the most anticipated event in our lifetime. It's so secretive we can't even get into the auditorium until one hour beforehand, but I can tell you by the size of this crowd, there won't be an empty seat in the house. It's estimated that over four billion people from all over the world will be watching this unprecedented telecast."

Chapter 48

The sun was setting on the city of Memphis when a large limousine pulled up to the rear of the auditorium. Benjamin Stone stepped out of the driver's side and opened the rear door for Vernon and Lisa Marie. Dave Carson was standing on the curb and greeted them as they emerged.

"Glad you made it," Dave said to Vernon.

"I don't know what we're doin' here, Dave, but I trust you. So, what's goin' on?"

"Just follow me," Dave said, and he escorted them inside. He patted Lisa Marie on the head. "How you doin', little darlin'?"

"I'm okay," she replied as she reached for her grandfather's hand.

Dave led them to a small lounge in the backstage area where Richard had been waiting for their arrival. He had gone over this conversation in his mind many times and could never figure

279

out exactly the right way to approach it. He felt such remorse for the heart-wrenching pain he had inflicted on these two for the past year. To let them think their son and father had died was hard to live with. He told himself he was helping them in the long run, but he still wrestled with the tactics they had taken to achieve their goal. He hesitated a moment and then slowly stood to address them. "Good evening, Mr. Presley. I'm Richard—"

"I know who you are," Vernon interrupted. "Good evening to you, Mr. Hart. So who's gonna tell me why we're here?"

"Could you sit down?" Richard motioned Vernon to have a seat and then looked to Lisa Marie. "Dave, could you take Lisa Marie to the dressing room?"

"Take her where?" Vernon asked.

"It's okay, Vernon," Dave assured him. "You'll see her in a few minutes." He then led Lisa Marie out of the lounge and toward a nearby dressing room.

"Mr. Presley," Richard said. "I don't know how to say this other than to just say it." He nervously fiddled with his Buffalo nickel and cleared his throat. "Your son...um—Your son is alive, and he's right down the hall."

"Come again?"

"Your son didn't die in that explosion. He's here."

Vernon stared at Richard for many long seconds and then exploded. "Is this a damned joke?" He jumped up from his chair, pointed at the young man, and yelled, "This is the cruelest thing anybody could pull."

"Mr. Presley, I'm not joking."

"Where's my granddaughter? Bring her back here!" Vernon demanded. "We're getting the hell out of here!"

"Please follow me," Richard motioned to him. He had never imagined the conversation would go well, but this had been worse than expected. He couldn't hand Vernon back off to Dave fast enough. "I'll take you to her."

Dave had walked Lisa Marie to a nearby dressing room and opened the door. "Lisa, there's someone in here that wants to see you." He waited for her to enter, and then he closed the door behind her and took a chair next to the door in the hall.

"Hello, is somebody here?" Lisa Marie quietly asked as she stepped into the room.

Elvis was seated in a chair on the other side of the room and watched in the mirror as his beloved daughter entered the room. He watched as she slowly walked forward, and it took his breath away when she made eye contact with him in the mirror. He watched her face light up and saw tears begin to fall down her cheeks.

"Daddy? Is that you?"

"Yes sweetheart, it's me," he said, and he swiveled the chair around to face her. "I've missed you so much, punkin." She ran to him, and he stood up and caught her in his arms. She hugged him tightly around the neck, and they both cried and laughed as he spun her around the room.

"I don't understand..." she said. "I don't un-derstand...is it really you?

"It's really me, darlin'. And I'll never leave you again. I promise."

"But Daddy, how?"

"Sweetheart, it's a long story," he said, sit-ting down with her in his lap. "I was given a sec-ond chance to be a better person—a better father and a better son. And I had to go away for a bit to make those things happen." He hugged her again and quietly said into her ear, "I'm so sorry for all the things I've done wrong. I promise you'll always be number one in my life. Nothin' will ever get in the way again."

While Elvis and Lisa Marie were inside the dressing room, Dave waited on the other side of the door. He could hear Vernon before he could see him.

"Where's Lisa Marie? We're leaving right now!" Vernon yelled as he and Richard rounded the corner.

"Vernon, calm down," Dave said, and he opened the door to the dressing room. "Just come in here."

Elvis was sitting at the dressing table, and Lisa Marie was in his lap, with her head buried in his chest. "Hey Dad," he said with a smile when he saw his father walk in.

"Who the hell are you? Put down my granddaughter!"

"Dad, it's me," Elvis said, and his face dropped. He hadn't expected this reaction.

"This is not my son," Vernon said to Richard and Dave. "Let go of my granddaughter!" he yelled at Elvis. "Lisa, let's get out of here." Vernon then looked back at Richard and Dave. "And I don't ever want to see you guys again."

Elvis stood up, put Lisa Marie back down, and walked over to his father. He put his hands on Vernon's shoulders.

"Get your hands off of me!" Vernon pushed Elvis' hands away.

"Dad, could you just please look at me?" Elvis pleaded. He grabbed his father and shouted, "Look at me!" When Vernon finally looked at him, Elvis said, "It's all true...I had to go away. My whole life was a mess. I'm so sorry. Can you forgive me?"

Vernon stared into Elvis' eyes for a few moments and then began to cry. "It's my son," he said quietly. "Son, it is you," Vernon said as he wiped his tears. "You've come back to me. Praise the Lord in heaven."

"You got that right," Elvis said, and the two men hugged each other very tightly as they both broke down and sobbed.

"I...I don't understand," Vernon's voice cracked.

"After this thing tonight, I'll explain everything to you at Graceland."

Vernon looked Elvis up and down. "You look so different."

"I'm off of everything. I'm clean—I feel great. I won't disappoint my family again. I'm gonna make you and Lisa Marie proud of me."

"Thank you Jesus, thank you," Vernon said, and then he hugged his son close again.

"Elvis, it's time," Richard interrupted. "We've got to go."

"Hold on, Richard. I'll be there in just a sec."

"No problem. Take your time."

"Darlin', Dad," Elvis looked at the two people he loved most in this world. "You ready to watch this old man shock the world?"

"What?" Vernon asked. "You're the May 24th? You're The Event?"

"That would be me." Elvis grabbed Lisa Marie's hand and placed his other arm around his father's shoulder. "Come on, y'all, come with me."

When they got back to the lounge area, he handed them off to one of the staff, who escorted them to the side of the stage where a special seating area had been arranged to provide them with a perfect backstage view. Elvis couldn't resist spying on his old band for a few minutes, so he hid out of view and watched them setting up. They were on stage behind the drawn curtain, doing sound checks and prepping for the performance. The drummer was working with the sound man, but put down his sticks abruptly and said, "Hey, it's Vernon and Lisa Marie. What are they doin' here?"

"It is an Elvis charity, stupid," the guitar player teased.

"Oh right," the drummer said, and he picked up his sticks again to resume where he had left off but then put them back down. "I thought I saw that rich dude earlier, Richard Hart. Did anyone else?"

"Yeah, man. That's who it was. I saw him too," the guitar player said.

"Would you two knuckleheads get back to work, dadgummit," the keyboardist teased. "We used to play for Elvis, for heaven's sake. It's not like you've never seen anybody famous. Now pick your sticks back up dude and finish that sound check."

Elvis laughed to himself at their confusion and had a hard time pulling himself away. He was going to have some fun with these guys later, he thought.

Chapter 49

Richard and Elvis headed toward the stage area together. Richard had changed into a suit and tie and had been prepped for camera, as had Elvis. They were both perfectly polished from head to toe.

"Hey Elvis, I want you to meet a special girl," Richard said. "Now don't make me look like a fool. Remember, I'm Nick."

"I wouldn't do that."

* * * *

"Atalynn," Richard said when they approached her. She had been sitting in an out-of-the-way backstage area and had not witnessed any of the interactions between Elvis and his family. She was surprised to see how different Richard now looked in his suit and tie. He didn't look anything like the stagehand she had arrived with.

"Hey, Nick," she said. "Look at you. Wow, you look so different. What's going on?"

"I want you to meet somebody," Richard said, and he motioned to Elvis, who was having a hard time containing his laughter.

"That guy looks just like—" she started.

"Don't say it," Elvis interrupted. "Wayne Newton."

"No, you look just like Elvis," she said. She studied him for a moment, tilting her head to the side. "But you actually look better than he did. You're the best impersonator I've ever seen."

"He's not really an impersonator," Richard said.

"Well he should be. He looks just like Elvis."

"Atalynn…there's…um…" Richard stammered. "There's something I've got to tell you, and I'm really afraid of what you're going to say, but it's time you found out." He looked down at the floor and then slowly back up at her.

"Come on buddy, gather your wits. It's gonna be okay," Elvis said.

"Nick, you're scaring me," Atalynn said. "What is it?"

"My name…my name isn't Nick. It's Richard Hart."

"What did you say?" she asked.

"It's Richard Hart."

"Don't kid with me like that, Nick. It's not funny."

Richard merely stared at her, and she could tell it was no joke.

"Are you serious?" she asked in disbelief. "The Richard Hart? My boss Richard Hart? No way."

"Please don't be mad. Let me explain," he said, and then he nudged Elvis. "Say something. Help me out here, man. You got me into this, now get me out."

"Alright then, I'll try. Darlin', I've known this guy here since he was ten years old. And I can tell ya, I've met a lot of people in my life, and he's one of the good guys. He's right, you know; I am the one that got him into this. He was only taking my advice with you. It's all my fault. Give him the break he deserves."

"I'm really confused. You're not really Elvis Presley, are you?"

Elvis turned so he was facing her sideways and pointed at her in his iconic stance. "The one and only."

Atalynn was taken aback. The man really was the spitting image of Elvis. She then looked back at Richard and suddenly felt as though she didn't know him at all. "You know what Nick—

Richard—whoever you are. I'm leaving," she said, and she turned toward the exit.

"Hey, hey, come here darlin'." Elvis gently grabbed her arm. "Don't do this to him. You have no idea what he's done to save my life. Give the man another chance. Please. He gave it to me."

"Whoever you are, I was falling for that guy, and I thought I knew him, but it looks like I didn't know him at all."

"How 'bout you do me a favor," Elvis said. "You go sit in the front seat like he wants you to and just give us five minutes. Please."

She sensed sincerity in his eyes, and the sound of his voice was so familiar. "You *are* Elvis Presley," she said as it dawned on her. "And you're the friend he was trying to help, aren't you?"

"Well of course, darlin'," Elvis said.

"Okay, I'll do it," she said to Elvis with a smile, and then she scowled at Richard.

"Atalynn, I'm so sorry for lying to you," Richard said. "Please just let me take you to your seat. If you can just hold off for a few more minutes, everything will become clear."

"Okay Nick—I mean Richard," she said, and she felt herself being drawn back in by his charm. "This better be good," she finally said, promising herself she'd make him work a bit harder to win her back. But she knew the battle had already been won. He tried to take her hand, but she brushed him aside.

"Come on, baby," he said with a forlorn look. "Follow me." He led her to the left side of the stage and pointed out an empty chair in the middle of the first row. She took her place center stage and introduced herself to the man who sat next to her.

* * * *

It was Lane Bishop she spoke with, and he was curious what part she had played in this; after all, everyone else seated nearby shared a connection to the story in some fashion. Beside Lane sat the little boy who had found Elvis' ring, accompanied by his mother, and on the other side of Atalynn sat Joel Cooper and his family. Lane suspected there was a story behind the beautiful girl who had just introduced herself, but that would have to wait for another day.

He was distracted from that thought when the little boy leaned over to him and asked, "Hey mister, you find that place where I found the ring?"

"Yep, just where you showed me," he answered, and then he said quietly under his breath, "Oh yeah, did I ever. You have no idea."

Chapter 50

"Ladies and gentlemen, it's time," Richard heard the announcement reverberate throughout the auditorium, and a hush fell over the crowd as the lights dimmed. Richard's heart beat wildly in his chest from his spot behind the large velvet curtains that separated him from the thousands of people that filled the auditorium. He took a deep breath and walked through the curtains and approached a microphone in the center of the stage. A spotlight shone down on him and momentarily blinded him, and all he could see was the stage below his feet. As he looked out into the audience, he could see nothing but darkness. *You've got this*, he said to himself as he secretly reached for the Buffalo nickel he had hidden in his coat pocket. He stood up to the microphone and began.

"Good evening, I'm Richard Hart. For people who don't know me, I'm a businessman and an

Elvis Presley fan. So let me explain to you how big of a fan I really am…"

* * * *

Throughout the world, people listened to this introduction and wondered what in the world was to follow. In his living room near Nashville, Johnny Cash sat on a sofa next to his wife, June, watching the telecast. "Way to go, little Richard," Johnny said. "You did the right thing."

June's mouth dropped open, and she looked to her husband. "Did you know about this?" He didn't answer her question, but his laughter at her reaction aroused her suspicions even further. He turned his attention back to the television in an attempt to distract her, and together they both listened to Richard's story unfold. A few moments into the speech, though, June again looked toward Johnny. She cocked her head, squinted her eyes, and shook her head in amusement. "You sly dog," she teased as she slapped him on the shoulder. "You did know about this."

He gave a slight nod of his head, and with a glint in his eyes, he winked at her and held a finger to his lips. He then wrapped his arm around her shoulder, and together they watched in anticipation as Richard continued to reveal the details of the elaborate plan.

* * * *

"...I kept this all a secret, even from my closest friends," Richard continued, "and the people I love, because this extraordinary event was to fulfill my father's wishes by saving the life of the man who saved mine." His vision had become clearer at this point, and he could now see Atalynn in the front row smiling up at him. This gave him the courage he needed to continue with his story and reveal to the world what he had been a part of.

While Richard spoke in front of the curtain to the audience, the band was ready behind the curtain, waiting to perform. Elvis, dressed in black, walked in front of them and took his place center stage with his head down and his back to them.

"Wow, that looks like E ten years ago," one of them whispered to the others.

"Sure does, spittin' image of him."

Elvis silently laughed while he stood in front of them and listened to their whispers. After a few moments, he turned slowly around and watched as their jaws dropped. "Hey boys," he said. He laughed at their shocked faces but was soon overcome with emotions at the sight of the band he had missed during his long time away. "Keep it cool, guys," he said while fighting back tears. Elvis looked at the ashen faces of his band, and he could tell that they, too, were overcome with emotion and that they were having a hard time regaining their composure and focusing back on their instruments and the performance that was moments away. "We'll talk later tonight at Graceland," he said. "Now we've got to take care of business."

Elvis turned back to the curtain and waited for Richard to end his speech, but Lisa Marie ran up to him and tugged on his sleeve. "Sweetheart, we're about to start. Get back to Grandpa," he said, and he watched as she grabbed her necklace, broke it, and took something off of it. She then handed his TCB ring to him. "How did you...you know what? Tell me later. Love you so much."

"Love you too, Daddy," she said.

He remembered the shell he had tucked into his pocket and handed it to her. "Here's somethin' for you too, punkin," he said, and then he kissed the top of her head. She turned to go, and he pulled her back to him and hugged her real tight one more time before she ran offstage to join her grandfather.

Elvis saw that Benjamin and Dave were now standing next to Vernon. Elvis suspected Dave had explained everything to Ben, who was now standing with his head bowed. He noticed the man's lips were moving as if he were praying. Elvis thought back on all the times Ben and Dave had struggled with him and his demons, and he thanked God that Dave had gone through these extraordinary measures to save him.

"So let's just get to it," Elvis heard Richard finishing up his speech. "Here he is."

The curtains parted, and Elvis looked around at the familiar sight. He had played this auditorium often during his career. A flood of memories came back from his early years. The audience erupted and jumped out of their seats as he walked up to the microphone. The sound was absolutely deafening, but it was music to Elvis' ears. He had missed this connection with an audience. He was ever the performer and swiveled his hips in the tight, black leather pants which aroused excited squeals from the crowd. He reached for the microphone and pulled it off of its stand and swung it around in a circle, causing the fringe on the sleeve of his tight black shirt to flow out in its wake. He pointed the microphone to the band, and they slowly started to play "If I Can Dream." Elvis looked out at the audience and up to the balcony, where he knew all of the staff from the island was watching. He looked to the side of the stage and saw that Priscilla was now standing next to Lisa Marie. He mouthed the words "happy birthday" to her, and Priscilla smiled back and nodded. He thought how right the two of them looked together, and he yearned to rekindle the fires that still burned for the woman who had been the love of his life.

Elvis looked to the other side of the stage and watched Richard as he tossed his Buffalo nickel up in the air. He thought he saw a tear in the man's eye, and though the sound of the crowd was deafening, Elvis could have sworn he heard Richard say, "Thanks, Dad. We did it."

Elvis looked back up to the balcony and saw that the angel with the Memphis Tigers T-shirt and baseball cap now stood among the crowd. He smiled up at him and gave him a quick two-finger salute. The angel saluted back and disappeared. The band continued to play, waiting for Elvis to start. He placed the microphone to his lips and started to sing.

The crowd's screams faded away, and a strong, clear voice rang out in Elvis' head. "Come on now. It's time to go." Elvis looked up to the balcony again and saw the angel motioning to him. A strong pulling sensation overtook him, and he felt himself being pulled away from the stage and out of the theater.

He found himself in a thick mist, and standing next to him was the angel. The angel was radiant and wearing a brilliant white suit.

"I believe you're ready now," the angel said. "It's time to see your mama and your brother."

"What about my little girl? Was this all a dream?"

"Not all of it. Some dreams are more than merely dreams—they're visions, or messages, or lessons, or in your case a mixture of all of these. You wanted a second chance and forgiveness, and you got it. You learned what you needed to, and along the way, you helped others find their way. Richard and Atalynn get married, and they have three kids. They fill up that big old house. Coop, well, he's happy with his family, and he stays busier than ever, flying the rich and famous around. Lane defeats his demons, and he and Dave become great friends. They're working on projects for Richard around the world. Your dad, he'll be up here in a couple of years—won't be long now. And your little girl..."

The angel waved his hand, and a faint vision of Lisa Marie appeared in front of Elvis. She was on a horse, galloping along the grounds of Graceland. Her hair was flowing in the wind, and she was laughing. Elvis reached toward the vision, but it faded away.

"I'm sure the boss will let you go down there from time to time to watch over her. She grows up to be a beautiful woman and a great mother to your precious grandchildren. She'll make you very proud. And your fans—there's a piece of you that still lives in the hearts of every one of them."

Elvis smiled and nodded his head. "Cool. I'm ready now...let's go."

The angel placed his hand on Elvis' shoulder and led him toward a thick cloud. "Come on. Your mama and Jesse are waitin' down there just a spell." When they were almost out of sight, the angel placed out his hand, and a baseball cap appeared. He put the cap on his head, and the mist enveloped them.

Acknowledgments:

We would like to express our gratitude to all of those who helped us breathe life into this story. We would especially like to thank the following for their support and creative suggestions: Scott Herford, Ray Mamrak, Pete Farrell, Zac Hadden, Sharon Parker, and Timothy Plain.

We would also like to thank our family members who were gracious enough to let us name characters after them throughout the book.

Thank you to our test readers who helped us get this story into shape: Julie Garrison, Theo Williams, and Phil and Jeanie Grisham.

And thanks to our editor, Camille, who expertly poured over every line with a fine-tooth comb.

Thanks to the members of the Livermore Movie Buffs who gave us encouragement and suggestions along the way.

And lastly, thanks to Christine's mother, Lyndell Garrison, a retired teacher of thirty years, who lovingly read each chapter as it was put onto paper. Her insights and experience were instrumental in getting us through the process.

About the Authors:

George & Christine Gomez

George has worked as a psychiatric registered nurse for over 30 years and has extensive experience in the treatment of drug addiction and the effects of withdrawals. He is an avid golfer, a movie trivia buff and a lifelong Elvis fan.

Christine is a software developer for one of the nation's premier national laboratories. She loves to read and spend time with her family. Though George will forever be a Tennessean at heart, the couple currently reside in Christine's home state of California with their two dogs.

15977936R00174

Made in the USA
San Bernardino, CA
12 October 2014